WHERE IT ALL BEGAN

BLUE MOON #7

LUCY SCORE

Bloom books

Where it All Began

Cover by Kari March

ISBN: 978-1-945631-15-3 (ebook)
ISBN: 978-1-7282-8268-8 (paperback)

Published by Bloom Books, an imprint of Sourcebooks
P.O. Box 4410, Naperville, Illinois 60567-4410
(630) 961-3900
sourcebooks.com

lucyscore.com

090622

To my readers. You are beautiful and bright, and I'm thankful for you every day.
You also have excellent taste in literature!

1

Present Day

*P*hoebe Merrill liked to cry on her birthday. Each year, she allowed herself thirty full minutes of absolute solitude in which she could cry her eyes out with a mix of gratitude, grief, joy, and generally a very large glass of wine.

Today, on the very fine spring day of her fifty-fifth birthday, it was a chilled glass of a nice Prosecco that sat on the desk in her still new kitchen. It was a bright and airy space with country white cabinets and large windows that served up sweeping views of field and forest. A space that had been a long time in the making.

Phoebe wasn't the type of woman to shy away from the beautiful symmetry of life. This was the exact spot on which she'd loved and lost and loved again. She'd learned, in these fifty-five blessed years, that an ending was never an ending.

There were big plans in the works today. Plans that made

the peaceful background noise of farm country in the spring even more valuable now. In less than an hour, her sons would stampede through her front door, most likely bickering as they had since they were boys. They'd take her to lunch, regale her with stories of her grandchildren, and then tonight was the surprise party she wasn't supposed to know about.

But mothers always knew. Especially when they lived in a small town that broadcasts the goings-on of every resident's private life.

Tonight, she'd celebrate with loved ones, enjoying glasses of champagne, hugs from her beautiful grandbabies, and the laughter of good friends. But for now, in this quiet, private moment, her thoughts were of the two men she'd been lucky enough to love in this life.

Franklin, her husband and best friend, had been the one to buy her the oversized wine glass at her elbow and the one to design this home for her with input from her sons. The intention of the home was to hold their very large, very loud blended family on celebratory occasions.

John, her first husband—may he rest in beautiful peace—had given her the land on which the house stood and three wonderful sons for whom she felt alternating but equal pulls of pride and annoyance. John had been the soul mate she'd never expected, the surprise of her lifetime.

It had been fifty-five years filled with love, and Phoebe wasn't in any hurry to come to the end of it. She had children, grandchildren, a man who loved every damn thing about her —including the fact that she was too free with her advice— and friends that made her laugh until she had to pee and held her hand through every rough patch she'd ever faced. She lived in a community that bordered on commune. A town in which everyone was so wrapped up in everyone else's lives the residents were all family minus the DNA.

Her life was miraculous. And there wasn't one single thing she'd change.

With that comforting thought, Phoebe opened the folder on the desk and began her ritual. The sheets of notebook paper had been folded and unfolded so many times the creases were like canyons. The handwriting scrawled across them still heartbreakingly familiar as if a ghost was reaching out to touch her. It was an essay she'd never transcribed to typewriter, or later a computer, as she had dozens of others.

This one meant more because of the blue ink and leaning scrawl. This one was just for her.

She took a fortifying sip of wine and began to read.

Phoebe, my wife, my heart. When you read this, know that you have been the greatest miracle in my life. And as weighty a thing as that is, don't believe for a second that your life is dimmer just because mine has ceased.

It's past midnight. And all three of our boys made it home to see me before I make my final journey. I can feel my time slipping away and, while I hate having our sons see me like this—frail, sick, unable to take a single one of them in a wrestling match—I want them to understand that death is nothing to fear. It is part of our journey, and as I've come to believe, perhaps it is the most beautiful part.

The looming shadow of death, the promise of the beginning of the next adventure, makes a man consider his life, his regrets. There's one I fear, one that keeps me awake even now. One that you have the power to save me from. I need to ask something of you that might sound impossible now, but I'm confident that with the healing power of time and the mule-headed commitment of our town, you will rise again, love again.

I need you to be someone else's miracle.

That heart of yours can't stop its gifts after I've returned to the earth and the air that I've loved so much in this lifetime. That would be an injustice. You are young. You are beautiful. You are brilliant. And someone out there is going to deserve your heart and mind even more than I ever did. Hiding from that, allowing grief to rob you of future happiness, would be my one and only regret.

So, please, Phoebe, don't let that happen... or I'll haunt you forever.

I've thought a lot about our life together these past few weeks. Being immobile and staring up at the fluorescent lights does that to a person, I suppose. I decided that between needles and nurses and the constant beep of machines more concerned with quantity than quality, I'd pinpoint the exact second that I knew you were it for me. That there wasn't another breath I'd want to take without you by my side.

This is where it all began...

PLANTING

2

June 1985

The lemon-yellow Triumph kicked up a cloud of dust behind it as Phoebe maneuvered the slow curves and easy hills of upstate New York's country roads. She glanced down at the map on the seat next to her, the path marked with highlighter, and hoped to God she was headed in the right direction. She'd just driven through a town that looked as though time had frozen it in the mid-sixties. Bell bottoms, tie-dye, and, by her count, eight VW vans parked around the main square. It was so authentic she wondered if they were shooting a movie in town.

She'd have stopped to poke around if she'd had the time. The video and record shop looked like it might house some treasures, and the bakery with its vibrant pink awning tempted her. But she was already running late, a sin in her book. If she was going to spend most of the summer on a man's farm picking his brain, the least she could do was show up on time.

Phoebe nearly missed the drive. The broken-down fence

that lined the road split for a sliver of dirt lane. A hand-painted sign hung crookedly from an unpainted post.

Pierce Acres read the wry script.

She bumped down the lane, swerving to miss the biggest of the ruts until the farm came into view and was relieved to find that there was indeed a house on the property. It was a traditional two-story that had seen better days. The serviceable white clapboard siding was clean, and the roof looked brand new, but the porch bowed and sagged, and the flowerbeds were overgrown with weeds. Phoebe noted there were no curtains in any of the dingy windows, though privacy didn't appear to be an issue out here with no neighbors for a quarter mile in each direction.

Across the drive from the house sat a dilapidated barn in faded red, though the fence around the scrap of land in front of the barn was new and freshly painted. The barn itself looked like a good stiff breeze would have it tumbling in on itself.

There was no welcoming committee visible, so she turned off the car and hefted her suitcase and typewriter out of the trunk. When she slammed the lid, the first signs of life stirred. A frantic yip came from the screen door on the porch. It bumped open an inch, closed, and then bumped again. A brown and white mottled dog the size of a toaster oven shoved its nose through the opening and muscled its way out.

"Hey, buddy," Phoebe said, dropping her baggage and sinking down. The dog hunkered down in suspicion and inched forward. It gave her hand a careful sniff and must have downgraded her threat status because he flopped on his back inviting a belly rub.

It was character that made the dog cute, not anything physical, Phoebe decided. He had one eye, an ear that flopped up, and an obscene length of tongue that lolled from the side of his mouth.

"Lousy guard duty, Murdock." The voice as rough as the gravel beneath her knees came from over her shoulder in the direction of the barn. Phoebe rose and then froze.

Farmers did *not* look like the man ambling toward her. They were older, weathered, craggy.

This guy looked like he'd walked off the set of *Dukes of Hazzard*. His dark hair was long, curling a bit at the ends. Grey eyes peered at her from a tanned face that carried a rough layer of stubble. His long, muscular legs were encased in tight denim. The dirty plaid shirt was tight across a set of spectacular biceps that bulged as he hefted two buckets filled with what looked and smelled like shit.

The man made carrying shit sexy. She'd had no idea that was possible. Now, if he was as smart as he was hot, her summer had just gotten a hell of a lot more interesting.

"John Pierce?" she asked, one-eyed dog and bags forgotten.

The man set the buckets down and peeled off his work gloves before offering her a large, callused hand. "That'd be me. And you are?"

Phoebe blinked, returning his strong grip. Just how many visitors was this farmer expecting? "I'm Phoebe. Phoebe Allen, the grad student you said could spend the summer."

He looked at her blankly.

She tried again. "Thesis? First generation farms and the obstacles they face post-farming crisis?" John was staring at her as if she'd just announced she was here to perform a craniotomy on him. Maybe he was daft? Maybe he'd hit his head on a piece of farming equipment and had lost his short- or long-term memory, whichever held the information that she was coming to stay with him for the summer and interview him for her thesis.

"*Phoebe* Allen?"

"Uh-huh."

He finally released his grip on her hand and swiped an arm over his forehead. "Son of a bitch."

"I beg your pardon?" It wasn't that Phoebe was opposed to bad language. She was a bit of a connoisseur of four letter words. But to lead an introduction with it was odd and didn't bode well.

"I was told you were a grad student named Allen."

She tilted her head to the side. "Technically I am."

"I was told you were a man."

"Who the hell told you that?"

"A meddling, exasperating liar, that's who." He was scowling now, his expression dark.

"Let me guess. You have a problem with me being a woman." Phoebe was used to the attitude. She was the only woman out of fourteen master's students in her class at Penn State University and one of only three in the entire College of Agriculture.

"Of course I do."

Phoebe settled her hands on her hips and drummed her fingers against the denim of her skirt. "Just because I'm young and female and a little on the short side doesn't preclude me from an interest in farming economics and rural sociology." She was gearing up to launch into her just-because-I-have-a-vagina lecture when he gave a short laugh.

"That's not what I meant."

"Then what did you mean?" Phoebe was toe-to-toe with him. Given the contents of the buckets he'd been hauling, she probably should have kept her distance, but she was mad enough, annoyed enough, to forget about her sandals and bare toes.

"I mean we can't live under the same roof all summer alone together."

Phoebe, never at a loss for words, found herself struggling to come up with any at the moment. "What? Why not?"

"I'm a single man. You're a single woman. We're not shacking up."

Phoebe looked over both shoulders. She had to be on one of those *Candid Camera* TV specials. "Do you have a calendar?" she asked finally.

"Not on me."

"It's funny because I could have sworn that it was 1985, not 1955. And that respectable, responsible adults who are *working* together don't need chaperones."

"You have no problem staying with a man you just met on a farm where the only witnesses to your potential screams would be a handful of chickens and a cow with a limp?"

"What kind of screams are we talking about? Murder or sexual?"

He didn't look amused. John was back to quietly staring at her, his gray eyes nearly silver in the softening light as day wound down into evening. She tipped her head back. "This would be a lot easier if you had a sense of humor."

"This would be a lot easier if you were a man."

"Look, John. Can I call you John, or should I stick with Mr. Pierce?" She didn't wait for an answer since he probably wouldn't get the joke anyway. "I'm an adult. I'm twenty-three years old, not a virgin, and not looking to do anything this summer but work on your farm and my thesis.

"If you don't think you can control yourself around me, say so now, and I'll scramble to find another guy who just decided 'Farming crisis, schmarming crisis. I think I'll start a first gen produce farm and carve out a living after thirty percent of my brethren got foreclosed upon in the last five years.' Shouldn't be a problem. Shouldn't throw off my thesis or push back my graduation at all and ruin my chances for a job in August."

Sarcasm was another one of her finer qualities that John Pierce obviously wasn't going to appreciate.

"I don't like being manipulated into things," he said.

"Who does?" Phoebe shrugged. "But if anyone did any manipulating here, it wasn't me, and I resent being held accountable for someone else's bad behavior."

He studied her quietly, and Phoebe felt a little tingle race from her toes to the roots of her hair. She held her breath. She was so close to graduation, so close to a job that excited her, so close to finally making things right for her parents. She wasn't going to let John Pierce—handsome devil or not—or anyone else wreck those plans.

Murdock let out a yip at John's feet. His stump of a tail wagged in the dirt.

"Guess it's close to supper time," John said, squinting up at the sun as it eased toward the horizon in the west. He looked back at Phoebe, and she squirmed under his amusement. "Guess you'll be wanting a place to put your suitcase."

"I guess so," she said, debating whether or not she should apologize for jumping down his throat. She was used to the razzing—and sometimes outright harassment—that came from her classmates and had come to expect it as an annoying downside to her chosen path. Technically, John didn't seem *as* concerned about a woman being interested in farming. He was more concerned about sharing a house with one, which to her was just as stupid.

"You gonna yell at me if I carry your suitcase?" he asked blandly.

Phoebe blew out her breath. "I think I can hold back on my verbal insults for the moment."

He leaned around her and picked up the case. "Can't ask for more than that. I'll show you Allen's room."

Had the serious farmer just make a joke? Was he relenting and inviting her to stay? Phoebe couldn't tell on either count.

Murdock bolted toward the side door of the house and scratched at the screen, and John set off in the same direction at a more leisurely pace. Phoebe hefted her typewriter case and followed along behind him.

The kitchen was small and dark and hadn't been redone since the 1950s. The refrigerator was original. The stove was a little newer, definitely an early 70s model in the same pea green as her suitcase. Orange and white linoleum tiles peeled up at the corners. The Formica dining table was a hand-me-down with rusty metal legs and a scarred top. Its four chairs boasted mismatched vinyl patterns of flowers, birds, and checkers.

"It's a, uh, work in progress," John said, looking around as if seeing his own kitchen for the first time.

"It's nice," she told him and meant it. The space was clean, and it was in better shape than her apartment off campus. Phoebe spent most of her time in the library, the lab, or the fields. Her shabby studio apartment was reserved for sleeping... and the occasional bottle of wine. This place felt like a home. An outdated home in desperate need of some sprucing up, but a home nonetheless.

Phoebe peered into one of the front rooms and discovered a dining room with peeling brown-on-brown graphic wallpaper that probably made dinner guests dizzy. Though judging by the fact that the room housed a table and no chairs, Phoebe assumed John didn't do much entertaining. Opposite was a small living room with requisite couch and recliner. "How long have you lived here?"

"Bought the place a year ago. Should have seen it then. It was a real wreck."

Before she could clarify if he was joking, John disappeared down the hallway toward the front of the house. She followed and grinned wistfully at the wallpaper here, black with orange and yellow flowers. It was a twin of the paper that had been in her grandmother's laundry room on the family farm. She'd have to dig her Polaroid out of her bag and snap a picture to send to her grandparents.

She followed John's remarkable denim-clad ass up the staircase and into a bedroom at the front of the house. It was small but cozy. There was a twin bed with a wrought iron headboard and no sheets near a dusty dresser that was missing four knobs, and she imagined the skinny door with the glass knob was a closet.

John stared at the bed for a long minute. "I don't have sheets." He sounded baffled as if bedding hadn't occurred to him when he'd agreed to house a guest.

So, he was going to let her stay the night at least, she thought, relieved. "That's okay. I've got my sleeping bag in the car." Phoebe prided herself on being a low-maintenance woman. She wore her long hair straight so she didn't need to deal with the case of Aqua Net most of her friends went through in a month. Her clothes were mostly variations on a theme: denim and cotton. And she was perfectly comfortable sleeping on a bare mattress or the floor of a tent.

"Bathroom's back that way." John jerked his thumb over his shoulder. "I'm across the hall. I'm going to grab a shower, and then maybe we'll figure out what to do with you. If you need anything just holler." He was gone before she could respond.

She smirked at his choice of words. Holler. Yep, she was definitely in farm country and with a farmer of few words. It was fine with her. Phoebe had more than enough words to make up for John's lack.

The springs sang as she sank down on the mattress. She plumped the lone pillow and flopped back against it and wondered if John really believed he had a choice about her staying.

3

———

What in the hell had he gotten himself into? John shook his head under the lukewarm water that trickled from the showerhead. He added "give the water heater another kick" to his list of immediate fixes.

He'd been mentally prepared to share his summer with Allen the grad student. Allen *the man*. He'd talk to him about the ins and outs of a small family farm. And in return, Allen would lend a much-needed hand in the fields. It was a simple, mutually beneficial arrangement that had just gone to hell.

Phoebe Allen, with her pretty bottle green eyes and long hair the color of deer hide, was not what he'd signed up for. And he knew exactly who had set him up. John was familiar with the mutterings from Blue Moon Bend's older generation. They were concerned about his well-being. Twenty-eight, living alone on two hundred ramshackle acres, unmarried? He scrubbed the grit and grime off his knuckles with more violence than necessary.

He *liked* his life. His *quiet* life on his very own plot of land. Here, it was one step at a time, moving with nature. He wasn't boxed up in some cubicle being a yes man and shuffling mounds of paperwork, worshipping a clock, and praying for vacation days. Here he had the greens of the grass, the whisper of the breeze through the leaves, skies that went on forever. Every day in nature was a vacation. And for company, John had Murdock and the frogs in the creek.

In fact, John thought bitterly as he swiped shampoo through his mop of hair that he'd been meaning to cut, he wasn't quite sure what had him agreeing to house a grad student for a few weeks in the first place. He could have gotten the help he needed just as easily in trade with another farmer.

He was just the latest victim of Blue Moon's mojo.

"Must be tough out there all by yourself on that farm. You could probably use some help, couldn't you?"

He'd thought at the time that she was referring to a farm hand. But it was clear as day now that she'd meant a wife. It was a known fact that if anyone was single in Blue Moon long enough, they'd be fixed up and married off before they knew what hit them.

And Mrs. Nordemann had pulled the trigger on him.

Grabbing for the soap again, he went over their conversation in his head.

"An excellent student—strong, smart, good head for numbers," Jillian Nordemann, who had married at nineteen and made it her mission in life to shove everyone else into the same wedded bliss, had practically glowed while reciting the assets of her second cousin's kid in grad school. "You could use some help around the farm. An extra pair of hands. You won't regret it. That I guarantee," she'd insisted.

He couldn't recall her using the very important pronoun that would have tipped him off to the fact that "he" was a "she."

It wasn't that John had anything against dating or marriage or even the very attractive woman in his guest bedroom. He just wasn't ready. He didn't need a girlfriend or a wife right now. He needed a capable pair of hands to get him through the summer on the farm. The water sputtered once, signaling the end of the hot water supply, and he twisted the knobs. This house wasn't much of a home, and when he was ready to find Mrs. Pierce, he'd damn well want to present her with something more than a shitty farm house, a falling down barn full of rusty equipment, and a meager crop yield.

He had plans. Goals. He wasn't about to drag someone in on the ground floor. And if he *were* ready, that woman would not be Phoebe Allen. She was too smart-mouthed, too opinionated, too busy. She would turn his quiet, comfortable life into chaos.

He wanted to use his two hands to build his future and didn't need anyone else interfering with the decision-making. John hated being maneuvered into a decision he'd rather not make, and it looked like Mrs. Nordemann and Phoebe had accomplished just that.

He ran a threadbare towel over his hair and across his chest and caught the grimness in his own expression in the mirror.

He'd known it was only a matter of time before someone meddled in his life. He shouldn't be surprised. He was a life-long Blue Mooner. And if he were inclined to act like it, he'd just scheme right back. He felt the upward turn in the corner of his mouth as he scrubbed a hand over the stubble he hadn't gotten around to shaving for the last few days.

Maybe he'd give them exactly what they wanted?

He'd give Phoebe the unforgettable, hands-on farm experience she demanded, and the second she cried uncle, he'd send her packing to Mrs. Nordemann's front door. If he ruined Mrs. Nordemann's attempts at a fix-up, he could buy himself at least a year before she wrangled another candidate for the future Mrs. Pierce.

He'd be back to his solitude in no time.

JOHN CHANGED into his last pair of clean Levi's and a t-shirt he found on his bedroom floor that smelled vaguely fresh and headed downstairs where he found Phoebe making herself right at home. Her fancy electric typewriter took up half the kitchen table. She wiggled out from under the table on her hands and knees. Her denim skirt rose higher and higher on the curve of her rear end as she made her way out. She didn't wiggle far enough and cracked the top of her head on the underside of the table.

"Shit!"

He smirked from the doorway and watched as she sat down in the chair, rubbing her head. She flicked a switch, and the typewriter hummed to life.

"Ahh," she sighed, satisfaction blooming on her face.

Great. Not only was she a woman. She was a nerd. John had landed himself the least helpful farm hand in the history of the industry.

"You hungry?" he asked abruptly.

Phoebe must not have heard him come in. She responded with a shriek and a jerk that sent papers flying.

John silently bid farewell to the temple-like quiet of his home.

"You scared the hell out of me!" She slapped a hand over her heart.

"Did you assume I'd never come back downstairs?"

"No. I..." She was glaring at him and seemed to have lost her thread of the conversation.

He glanced down wondering what distracted her. He was indeed wearing pants, and he couldn't see any gruesome stains that would hold a woman captivated. "What?" he demanded.

Phoebe blinked and closed her mouth. "Nothing. You were saying something about... something?"

"I was asking if you were hungry. Normally I just have a sandwich for supper, but I could be talked into pizza tonight."

"Pizza?" There was a hopeful quality in her tone.

"Pizza, and we can talk about this... arrangement."

The smug look on her face told him that Phoebe assumed she'd won.

4

-----

*P*hoebe eased her butt onto the ripped upholstery of the passenger seat in John's elderly pick-up truck. She was trying to keep her knees glued together beneath the restrictive denim skirt so John wouldn't get an unnecessary view of her underwear. *Of course,* he'd insisted on opening her door for her. That's what 1950s etiquette dictated.

He shut her door soundly before she could remind him that she was perfectly capable of opening and closing her own doors. It was probably for the best. She needed to keep her lectures to herself until she was sure he was going to let her stay. He may have shown her a bedroom, but that didn't mean he wasn't going to show her the door in the morning.

She should have changed into jeans first, but she'd felt that might have been too presumptuous of her. She wasn't opposed to presumption when it played in her favor, but she couldn't get a read on the man. And any action she took could result in him sending her packing, putting her thesis in danger.

So, she'd settled for sending a subtler message, staking her claim by setting up her typewriter on John's kitchen table.

He slid behind the wheel, and in the enclosed space, she

caught a pleasing whiff of his soap. The ends of his hair were still damp from his shower, curling at the back of his neck. Physically, he ranked right up there with Hollywood's finest hunks. Broad shoulders, tight jeans, a sexy face with chiseled lines, and a glorious crop of stubble. His eyes were serious, searching.

John Pierce was enough to make any woman pause to take in the view—as she had when he'd strolled into the kitchen—but Phoebe wasn't quite ready to rule him the sexiest man she'd ever laid eyes on. Her level of attraction to a man depended heavily on character and intelligence, both of which had yet to be determined.

"Are we going into the town that time forgot?" Phoebe asked, securing her seatbelt.

The corner of John's mouth turned up as he turned the key and shifted into reverse. "I take it you drove through Blue Moon on your way here."

"What's the story there?"

"Story?" he asked, as they bumped along down the lane.

She rolled her eyes skyward. "A place like that doesn't *not* have a story behind it."

"You ever hear of Woodstock?" John asked.

She shot him a cool look. "It sounds vaguely familiar." There was that quirk in his lips again. *Jerk.*

"Well, after Woodstock wrapped, everyone headed home. But not everyone made it. A dozen or more partakers got lost on their way back and ended up setting up camp in the town square. They liked the place so much they decided to stay."

"Just like that? They never went home?"

John shrugged his big shoulders. "Probably baked out of their gourds. I was twelve when they showed up, pitching tents, camping in VWs. The whole town smelled like grass." His laugh was warm with the memory.

"You're pulling my leg." She could see the edge of town up ahead and was anxious for it to reveal itself.

John shook his head and grinned at her. And Phoebe felt her stomach turn itself into knots. *Wow.* The man had a smile that could melt her Maidenforms right off her. She'd have to watch out for that. She was here for professional reasons, not to dip a toe into the local dating pool.

"I kid you not. They were so good-natured and 'make love not war' and 'free lovey' that no one in town minded them. We had a town meeting and decided to help them all resettle here. Most of them and their families still live here today. Blue Moon assumed the hippies would adapt to us, but as you can see," he said, pointing to a sprawling Victorian decked out in purple and pink. There were dozens of wind chimes hanging from both porches and a paint splattered school bus parked in the front lawn. "We were wrong."

"Is that decoration?"

"The Fitzsimmons think so," John said, with the lift of a shoulder. There was no judgment behind his tone. Just a casual acceptance of oddity.

It was too bad that he couldn't extend that acceptance to her, Phoebe thought.

"And everyone just went along with it?" she asked.

"We were just a tiny farming community before 1969. Now, we're practically a commune. You won't ever find a tighter knit town," he predicted.

She frowned as John slowed the truck and abruptly pulled over to the side of the road. Phoebe Allen was no one's fool, and they were *not* out of gas. But she kept her comments to herself when John slid out from behind the wheel and ambled around the front of the truck. She saw it then. Something slim and black on the road. A hose?

"Oh gross!" The hose moved as John approached.

She stuck her head out her window as John crouched down within what looked like striking distance. "What are you doing?" she demanded.

"Moving him off the road." John's voice was beyond calm. It bordered on bored.

"You're not going to touch it, are you?"

"Can you please stop shrieking? He doesn't like it." John stood up and Phoebe's eyes bugged out at the five feet of snake he held in his hands as casually as a garden hose.

"Don't let it bite you!"

"Harmless black snake," he called over his shoulder as he walked it across the street to the wooded gully. Phoebe wriggled out of her seat and sat on the window ledge to watch John over the top of the truck's cab.

She saw the hideous thing swing what was most likely its head in John's direction. He side-stepped it and deposited the snake in the tall grass.

"Harmless?" Phoebe asked.

"Won't kill you if it bites you," he clarified.

"But it would still bite."

He shrugged. John's equivalent of a retort.

He climbed behind the wheel again, and Phoebe slid back into her seat, her pulse still racing. "You just picked up a snake." She shook her head at the image. Her farmer was an idiot.

"He just needed a little help. They sun themselves on the road, and if someone came around too fast he'd have gotten hit." John shifted back into gear and the truck rumbled down the road.

A ha! The misguided hero type, Phoebe decided, studying his profile. He certainly looked the part. That was something she could work with.

Satisfied, she looked out her window at the town. And

then her skin began to crawl. She checked both of her feet and under the seat, knowing full well it was just psychological. She didn't miss the smirk on John's lips when she was finally satisfied there was no snake ready to take a bite out of her.

At least he was smart enough not to comment, she noted. Instead, he pointed out a sweet little cottage tucked into a wooded lot on her right with the word PEACE painted across its front in a rainbow.

"That's insane."

John leveled a look at her. "You haven't seen anything yet."

∼

NAMED in recognition of the endearing wandering hippies, One Love Park took up a whole block in the very center of town. There were signs staked into the ground at varying intervals.

Have you hugged a tree today?

Don't worry. Be hippie.

Clothing no longer optional.

Phoebe kept her nose glued to the window, afraid she would miss something, as John cruised down the block. He pulled into a slot on the end of the park between a movie theater and a pizzeria.

Peace of Pizza was impossible to miss with its bright purple awning. The windows were decorated with colorful bubble-lettered posters describing specials. She could see lava lamps burbling away inside.

"No. Way."

"No way to pizza?" John asked.

"Huh? No. I mean yes. I definitely want pizza. I just can't believe a place like this exists."

"Good, because our choices are limited. There's a custard place across the street, a diner on the other side of town, and a Wag's about ten miles south of here."

Phoebe's stomach growled. "Nope. Pizza is perfect."

She climbed out of her seat before John could make it around to open her door, but she wasn't fast enough to beat him to the front door of the pizza shop. She stepped inside and into sensory overload.

The usual pizza place scents of marinara and oregano enveloped her. But that's where typical stopped. The shop's walls, carpeted in orange shag, held black and white prints of the Woodstock greats. Jimi Hendrix, Joan Baez, Arlo Guthrie. There were a dozen tables, half of them occupied. Each table had its own lava lamp in blues and oranges, and the salt and pepper shakers, when sat side-by-side, formed green and white peace signs. Phoebe sniffed the air as a server carrying a pie with a tomato sauce peace sign squeezed past.

"What brings you off the farm tonight, John?" A woman with ebony, waist-length dreadlocks and the flawless skin of a Cover Girl model leaned against the hostess stand. She wore a dashiki in faded burnt oranges and reds.

"Got an unexpected extra mouth to feed," he said, jerking his thumb in Phoebe's direction. "Lebanon bologna wasn't going to cut it."

The way the hostess grinned up at him, Phoebe guessed that might have been a slice of John Pierce humor.

"Phoebe, this is Bobby. She owns this establishment and makes the best sauce in five counties. Bobby, this is Phoebe the farm hand/grad student I was misled to believe was a man."

Phoebe thrust her hand out to Bobby. "It's a pleasure to

meet you. Your shop is incredible, and I promise to enjoy it, even though I'm not a man." She sent John a glowering look over her shoulder.

Bobby shook her hand with a firm grip and a white-toothed grin. "Man or woman, you're welcome here."

"That's very *open-minded* of you, Bobby." Phoebe sent another pointed look in John's direction. "I appreciate that."

It was John's turn to roll his eyes.

Bobby guided them to a purple upholstered booth along the wall under a framed picture of Janis Joplin in all her round glasses and headband glory. Phoebe took the side with her back to the wall so she could enjoy the comings and goings of Peace of Pizza's patrons.

It was an eclectic crowd. Customers in business suits shared tables with others dressed in decades-old denim and faded 60s rock band t-shirts. There were more headbands than perms, and Phoebe realized that, for once, she fit right in with her long, straight hair. If John let her stay, maybe she could find one of those wide, tie-dye headbands. A souvenir, a memento of her summer here.

He had to let her stay, she thought, fingernails digging into her palms. *Everything she'd been working for was riding on him.*

John pushed his unopened menu to the edge of the table. "Pizza?" he asked, interlacing his long fingers on the table.

"Loaded?"

"Pepperoni," he countered.

"Pepperoni, sausage, and green pepper."

"Deal." He offered her his hand over the table. "Large?"

Phoebe accepted his hand and shook, trying not to enjoy the callused texture of his palm against hers. Her stomach gave an unladylike gurgle. "Definitely large." She set her menu aside and mirrored his posture. "You strike me as a man who values when someone gets to the point."

John didn't say anything to acknowledge that he'd heard her, but his eyes, reflecting the light of the turquoise bubbles in the lava lamp, held her gaze.

"Let me tell you exactly what you'd be getting by letting me stay for the summer," Phoebe insisted.

He unfolded his hands palms up. "By all means."

"I'm strong and have a ridiculous energy level. I only need six hours of sleep a night and work my ass off every damn day. I've worked on my grandfather's farm every summer since I was seven years old. I'm not afraid of hard work or heavy lifting, and I'm so close to finishing my master's degree that I can taste it. I just need a sliver of your time and some hands-on experience to make this happen. I need your help, John. I can't do it without you."

She put it all on the table and gave him her best pleading look. *Please, John.*

"My future is in your hands."

5

John was already regretting his decision when his feet hit the bedroom floor the next morning. The sun wouldn't be up for another hour yet. He could at least wrangle a little peace and quiet before his new "farm hand" woke up and started rattling off questions like a damned parakeet.

He'd told her she could stay, even voiced his "concerns" that the work would be too much for her. If Phoebe had picked up on his warning hint that he wasn't going to go easy on her, she'd brushed it off and looked at him with those glass green eyes, and he found himself nodding dumbly.

She hadn't thanked him profusely, tears glistening and lip trembling. She'd merely nodded smugly as if she'd expected that answer all along.

He'd at least had enough wits about him to put a trial period on it. She had until the fourth of July to prove herself to a) be helpful and b) not be a nuisance. She'd agreed and immediately forgot about b, demanding to know the story of every person present in Peace of Pizza.

He came home with a dull headache, one measly leftover

slice of pizza, and a house guest for the next two weeks.

John crept down the stairs determined not to wake Phoebe so he could at least have a cup of coffee in peace. He was debating whether he could get away with making that lone slice of pizza his breakfast when he realized the kitchen lights were already on.

"Morning," Phoebe called cheerfully from the stove where she was scrambling something in his one and only fry pan.

Goddamn it. Just half an hour of quiet. Was that too much to ask?

She nodded toward the coffee maker as it sputtered to life on the counter. "Best part of waking up," she said with the perkiness of a true morning person. John skirted around her and caught a whiff of his own shampoo in her hair.

He blamed his knee-jerk arousal on his lack of sleep and his foggy brain. He'd slept like the dead alone in this house for a year now. But Phoebe's presence across the hall—on his only set of sheets, no less—had dominated his brain for the majority of the night. He'd counted ceiling tiles for hours. There were one hundred and forty-four of them in his bedroom. He'd triple checked before finally falling asleep into a restless dream about green eyes begging for help.

"Hey, where's your TV? I poked my head into the living room, but I didn't see one."

"Don't have one," he said gruffly. And he was sure she'd have a thousand things to say about that. But he changed the subject before she could. "Did you sleep well?" John knew it was mean, but he hoped she'd slept like shit.

"Slept like there was a carbon monoxide leak in my room," Phoebe said, plating up fluffy yellow eggs. Two slices of bread popped up like a jack-in-the-box out of the jaundice yellow toaster his mother had given him when she and his father had packed up for their big move west.

She handed him the plates jerking her chin toward the table, and while he stared stupidly at the breakfast in his hands, Phoebe efficiently filled two thick handled mugs with coffee.

"So," she said, setting the mugs down on the table. "What are we doing today?"

He followed suit with the plates and pulled out a chair. John couldn't remember the last time he'd sat down for breakfast. Usually it was a bowl of cereal eaten standing up or a piece of toast on his way out the door.

He reached for his coffee with a twinge of desperation. "Feed the cow and turn her out."

"You mentioned a limping cow yesterday. Is she livestock?"

He shook his head. "She's a pet. She was a neglect case from over in Cleary," he said shooting his thumb over his shoulder in the direction of the neighboring town. "The vet needed a place to keep her while she healed, and I opened my big, fat mouth. Now Pierce Acres has a cow."

It was the most words he'd spoken pre-dawn in years. But it still wasn't enough for Phoebe.

"After our pet cow, what then?" She dug into the eggs with enthusiasm.

Maybe he could put Phoebe on shoveling out the grain bin that needed to be emptied while he handled the roadside mowing. He'd get some quiet time before lunch. If he gave her too much information up front, she'd be asking him questions about the sprayer apertures and his life goals while they were weeding the borders of his fields.

"Let's just start with Melanie and go from there."

She put her fork down. "You named your cow Melanie?"

The piece of toast stuck in John's throat. "She, uh, has these deep, soulful brown eyes. Reminded me of my girlfriend in high school."

Phoebe's laugh lit up the room brighter than the basket weave pendant light over their heads. "Does human Melanie know about her namesake?"

John swallowed hard, the coffee warming a path to his stomach. "I hope not. She moved away after she graduated from college. Married a dentist and lives in Milwaukee."

"So, Blue Moon isn't one of those small towns where everyone knows everything and someone didn't write Melanie a letter saying 'You'll never guess what John Pierce named his new cow.'"

Shit. That was exactly the kind of town Blue Moon was.

He rose and carried his dishes to the sink, guzzling the last of his coffee. "Let's get this day started," he grumbled.

HE STUCK *her in the grain bin on purpose*, Phoebe thought as her shovel scraped metal under the last dredges of grain. Her grandfather had done the same thing when he was tired of answering her incessant questions. But she couldn't help it. As a child, she'd been endlessly fascinated by every aspect of life, and adulthood had done little to dull her interest. It was interesting to note that her questions seemed to have the same effect on John as they did her grandfather: one word answers that devolved into grunts and then finally redirection.

She wondered if farmers by design preferred solitude. That kind of life would never suit her. She needed people and stories and connection. Squatting on a piece of land and only seeing your neighbors every other week when you rode into town for supplies sounded depressing. It was why she was more interested in the business of farming than the actual field work.

But there was something to be said for the satisfaction of

manual labor. The familiarity of the work, the shuffle and scoop motion designed to save lower backs, reminded her of summers that seemed to stretch on forever. Of her grandmother hanging wash on the line in the backyard, and strawberry preserves in neat rows on the cellar shelves, and the smell of her grandfather's pipe tobacco.

John thought he was torturing her with the menial task, but he was providing an unintended and very pleasant trip down memory lane.

So, she did what she'd done then, entertained herself by singing her favorite songs of the '70s. Her words, accented by the sharp slice of shovel, echoed all around her off the metal of the bin. There was barely a foot of grain left in the bottom of the bin, and she figured she could get about half of it fed through the auger before John came to check on her progress.

She switched from "I Will Survive" to an enthusiastic rendition of "Don't Stop 'Til You Get Enough," adding a little swing to her hips with each shuffling step forward.

"Didn't know this was *American Bandstand* in here." John's voice bounced off the curving metal walls, cutting off her superb solo.

"Didn't know someone without a TV could be up on pop culture," Phoebe quipped back. She paused in her shoveling to swipe an arm across her sweaty forehead. He'd given up on her solitary confinement sooner than she'd thought he would, and Phoebe felt a twinge of disappointment that she wouldn't be able to blow his mind with her shoveling prowess.

John eyed the floor of the bin and silently picked up the second shovel leaning against the wall. Together they dug back into the grain, and Phoebe gave the silence a few minutes. When it became unbearable, she started humming and soon after that returned to her homage to Michael Jackson.

John didn't join in. He didn't seem like the singalong type, but Phoebe noted that his shovel scoops were timed with her beat, and that made her smile. She stole glances as they circled in opposite directions and wondered dispassionately what made men doing physical labor so appealing.

The sinewy bulge of his biceps, the sweat stains on his t-shirt, the way his Levi's hugged those muscular thighs. All those parts added up to a pretty spectacular whole. She wasn't feeling so objective now, Phoebe noticed. But she'd never doubted John's physical attraction. What she'd yet to nail down was his analytical sex appeal. Was he kind? Smart? Funny? Interesting?

He was sending her mixed messages. First, he was beyond reluctant to welcome her into his life for the summer and made her beg to stay. Not a good start. Then, he'd stripped the sheets off his own bed and put them on hers. She'd fallen asleep wrapped in the scent of him, subconsciously finding it a comfort for her first night in a new place. Thoughtful and generous. But he treated her questions—and her presence—like a nuisance. Irritating and pompous.

To Phoebe, her questions served dual purposes. They gave her information that she sought for her thesis, and they added to her measure of the man. Unfortunately, John hadn't whole-heartedly committed himself to being the A to her Q's. Phoebe knew herself well enough to know she'd tolerate his intolerance only for so long before she set him straight. Currently she was pretending to be a polite houseguest, but with her entire future and her family's well-being in John's hands, she couldn't afford to stay politely patient.

She noticed the change in his pace. He was shoveling faster now, and she adjusted to match. Her breath was coming harder now, and the sweat was running freely, but Phoebe could pull her weight. She could hang with the big boys. She'd proven it before and wasn't opposed to proving it again to a new audience.

There was nothing on God's green earth that was going to make her stop first. Even when her low back gave a creaking warning and when she felt the definitive beginnings of blisters rising on her thumb and palm. She didn't stop until he took the shovel from her rigor mortis fingers.

"It's not a race," he said, looking amused.

"That's usually what guys say when I beat them." Her flippancy would have come off better if she wasn't so winded.

John tossed the shovel down and quick as lightning reached for her hands. He turned them palms up and examined the red welts. "First of all, a good job is better than a fast job. Secondly, a farm hand is only as valuable as the hand they're able to give," he said quietly.

"There's nothing wrong with being quick, and I can work through blisters," Phoebe protested.

"The point is you don't have to. You could have taken it slower, worn gloves, taken breaks," John pointed out. "Now, we have to stop what we're doing and go patch you up."

He was chastising her like a child, and Phoebe bristled at it.

"I'm perfectly capable of slapping on a few bandages just fine by myself. You don't need to be so inconvenienced."

He looked at her, his mouth grim. "There's a difference between rushing through something to get to the other side and doing it right."

"There's also something to be said for speed and efficiency over plodding," Phoebe shot back.

"Let's go," he said gesturing toward the doorway.

"Oh, after you," Phoebe insisted. She smirked at the tension in his shoulders as she filed out after him.

6

He wasn't exactly gentle when he put the bandages on her, but he didn't slap them in place either. And maybe he did take a little extra time smoothing the adhesive down, but that was more to annoy her than it was to enjoy the spark of awareness he felt every time he touched her.

"If I were Man Allen, would you be bandaging me up?" Phoebe demanded. She swung her legs impatiently from her perch on top of the table.

He raised his gaze from her palms to her face. She was annoyed. Good. So was he. "Man Allen probably wouldn't fuss about it nearly as much as you are." John tightened the lid on the mercurochrome and boxed up the unused bandages.

"I'm not fussing!"

"Now you're pouting," he pointed out, and before he knew what he was doing, he'd flicked a finger over her lower lip, which was most definitely protruding.

It felt like the kind of static shock from wearing thick socks on carpet in the winter. A discharge of energy, a spark. Whatever it was, they both felt it. John took a quick step back and busied himself with his meager first aid supplies.

Phoebe remained—thankfully—quiet. She looked down at his handiwork on her palms but said nothing.

He cursed himself. Being attracted to Phoebe was not part of the plan. In fact, it was the worst thing he could do. He didn't want to be sharing his home, his farm, his days with anyone. And the sooner Phoebe gave up and packed up, the sooner he could get back to his life just the way he liked it. Wanting her was out of the question.

He shoved the bandages and supplies back in the cabinet and looked at the clock on the wall. "Might as well have lunch while we're in here."

Phoebe slid off the table, suspiciously subdued. "Can I help?"

"If you promise not to get any blister pus in the sandwiches."

She blinked those wide eyes at him. "I'm sorry. Did you just make a joke?" She took four slices of bread from the loaf on the counter.

John handed her two plates and opened the refrigerator. "No. I really don't want you to get pus in my sandwich."

"Is it because you aren't around people very often that you don't know how to be funny?" she asked.

"I like being alone. There's no pressure to be anything other than what I am," he said pointedly.

"And what does my presence pressure you to be?" she asked, accepting the sliced turkey and American cheese he handed her.

"A babysitter," he said, before he thought better. "A host." *A polite human being who wears pants in the house even at night*, he added silently.

Her full lips curved at their corners. "Mayo or mustard?" she asked.

He reached over her, careful not to touch her again and retrieved two glasses from the cabinet above her. "Both." She was too pretty for his liking. He didn't *want* to be attracted to her. She'd gathered her hair in a braid that hung down her back. Her jeans fit her a little too well around the hips and her shapely ass. Her t-shirt said Culture Club across the chest and accentuated all the right curves. He tried to focus on the words rather than what was under the cotton. Culture Club was probably some ridiculous philosophical, question-asking society at Penn State. A club designed to pick apart human beings and sort them into categories, John decided. Phoebe was probably president.

She opened drawers until she found his pitiful selection of utensils and pulled out a knife.

With Phoebe rummaging around his home, it was becoming painfully obvious that he really needed to take care of some basic shopping for the house. Something he'd put off because what did he care if he only had one set of sheets, three mismatched towels and a handful of forks? It was another thing to add to the list of things he resented about her. Her presence was a constant reminder of just how far behind he was in making his house a home.

"Do you ever answer any question with more than one syllable?" she asked conversationally as she slathered the bread with mayonnaise.

"Do you ever do anything besides ask questions?"

She leveled a frosty look at him and set the knife down with a clatter. "I would like to be writing my thesis, but it's a little difficult without *answers!*"

"I don't know what you want from me."

"Answers, John. I want answers. Real ones. Not just 'yes, no, because.'"

So, there was a temper in there in addition to mule-headed stubbornness, John noted. It was a combination that should be off-putting to him. He didn't like temperamental, pushy women. And that was exactly what Phoebe was. Lecturing him in his own kitchen after he was nice enough to let her stay? He didn't go for drama, not in entertainment and certainly not in women.

And yet, as he watched her fume her way around the room muttering about obstinate men, he wondered why he was entertaining the idea of putting his hands on her and kissing her until she finally shut up.

It took eight days before Phoebe broke. Eight days of weeding, shoveling, mowing, painting, fixing, cleaning, scooping, and one-word answers before she cracked like a piñata at a 5-year-old's birthday party.

Getting answers out of John Pierce was like trying to pick a deadbolt with a toothpick. And she was getting tired of the splinters.

Phoebe had tried everything. Softening him up with meals, giving him what she deemed an appropriate amount of quiet time, leading with softball questions that she already knew the answers to. Nothing. Worked.

Prying more than a one- or two-word answer from John's mouth was impossible. It seemed the longer she was there, the quieter he became. And it was driving her in-freaking-sane.

She had so much riding on him. She *needed* this. The desperation was palpable. Her family was counting on her graduating this summer. There was no money for another semester of school, and it was time for her to repay the support her parents had so generously given her. It was her turn to make a difference in their lives.

She and John had finished up in the fields a little early today. The beautiful summer day offered up baby blue skies, cotton ball clouds, and absolutely no helpful conversation with John. After a shower and a change of clothes, Phoebe settled in at her typewriter with the scant notes she'd taken since her arrival. Every morning she woke confident that today would be the day she found a way over or around John's walls. And every night she went to bed frustrated.

They didn't have to be friends, damn it. She just needed him to help her out. What was so hard about talking to her?

The longer she stared at her notes, the higher her temper spiked.

And when John waltzed in—walked really, but she was annoyed enough to see only condescension in his stride—her fingers tightened on the pencil she held until she heard the crack.

He opened the fridge and grabbed a beer. "You want one?" he offered.

"No. Thank you," she said coolly.

"Something wrong?" he asked, leaning against the counter obnoxiously amused.

She pushed her chair away from the table and stood slowly. She'd give him one last chance. One last chance to redeem himself before she murdered him on the spot with his own beer bottle. "Why did you decide to let the field east of the woods go fallow?"

He leveled her a look that transmitted his annoyance loud and clear. "Felt like it."

And so began her rampage.

"Okay, that's it!" She closed the distance between them carried by temper. "What. Is. Your. Damage?" She drilled a finger into his chest—a solid wall of muscle—to accentuate every word.

"My damage?" He looked baffled.

"What is wrong with you? Are you incapable of communicating with other human beings? Do you hate having a woman under your roof that much, or is it just me that you can't stand?"

"Where is this coming from?" he asked, setting his beer down on the counter with reluctance.

"Oh, I don't know!" Phoebe threw her arms up in the air. "Maybe it's coming from the fact that you said I could stay. You knew what I needed. You are the reason I'm here, and you're treating me like I have leprosy."

"Do you have to argue about everything?" John asked, rubbing his fingers over his brow. His calm tone shoved Phoebe even further over the edge.

"Do you have to automatically dismiss everything I have to say?" Her voice was a full octave higher than usual, and at this point, she didn't give a damn. "I was invited here, then I had to beg you to let me stay. I could have spent the summer with my family or somewhere I'd be welcome, but no! I'm stuck here with you, the plodding, disinterested, stuck-in-the-1950s farmer! Do you think I enjoy being in a place where I'm not wanted? In a position of needing something from someone who obviously can't stand having me around? Do you think I like that?"

"Um. No?" John ventured.

"You're damn right no!" Phoebe glared at him until her vision turned red. She let out a groan of exasperation. If she didn't get out of this house right now, she was going to burn it down with him in it and not feel a lick of guilt as she merrily roasted marshmallows over his charcoaled corpse.

She stormed out of the kitchen and down the hallway. Her purse and car keys were on the rickety table just inside the door. She snatched them up and yanked open the front door.

"Phoebe, hang on," John called after her.

Her only response to him was a middle finger over her shoulder a second before she slammed the door behind her.

Phoebe stormed off the porch and slid behind the wheel of her Triumph. She took a tiny bit of pleasure at sending gravel flying as she tore down the lane. John Pierce wasn't the only one who could behave like a manner-less asshole.

She turned the wheel toward Blue Moon and let the late afternoon sun soak into her, hoping it would bake the anger out of her. God, she just needed a break to figure him out. She could crack him. She knew she could. She just hadn't found the right approach yet. Of course, screaming like a banshee at the man in his own kitchen probably wasn't her best choice, but he'd deserved it. The lout.

Phoebe reached over and cranked up her radio. This was nothing some good tunes and summer sunshine couldn't cure. And if that didn't work, she'd do a little shopping in town. And then when she got back to the farm...

Shit. She didn't have a key. He'd never offered her one, and though she wasn't sure John even locked his doors, what would she do if he locked her out? What if he'd just been pushing her to get her out?

"Damn it," she muttered to herself. If this was it in her relationship with John, her thesis was toast. Which meant she wouldn't be graduating in August. She'd need to track down another first-generation farmer and spend *another* semester researching, writing, polishing. By the time she graduated, the research stations position with the PA Department of Agriculture would have gone to someone else and her parents' house would be in foreclosure.

She could kiss her best laid plans good-bye if something didn't magically change in the next thirty minutes.

She turned onto Main Street and pulled into a parking space in front of a sprawling tri-level brick building. The sign said McCafferty's Farm Supply. She got out of the car and studied her options. She was in no mental state to browse farm supplies. The bakery was tempting as always, but it was the pay phone in the park that pulled her. She desperately needed to hear a friendly voice.

Phoebe emptied her change purse and fed the requisite quarters into the phone. It rang twice before Phoebe was rewarded with her sister's cheerful greeting.

"Hey, Rose."

"Oh, man. What's wrong?" her sister demanded.

Phoebe smiled even as her eyes filled with tears. "I miss you. Is that a crime?"

"No seriously, what's going on? How's the whole farm thing going?"

"It's like not going at all," Phoebe confessed. "I can't crack this guy. And I need this—*we* need this—so bad. I'm feeling desperate."

Her sister hmm-ed on her end. "What are you going to do?" Rose knew better than to offer Phoebe advice. They both were well-aware of the fact that Phoebe was the headstrong one, the sister who jumped first and worried about consequences after the fact. The sister who ignored well-meaning advice like it was background noise.

"I don't know. I basically just screamed at him and drove off in a childish but very satisfying temper tantrum." Phoebe rested her head on the foggy plastic surrounding the phone. "How's Dad doing?" she asked, changing the subject.

"The doctors seem pleased with his progress. But, as we guessed, going back to work is out of the question. I honestly don't see him ever going back." Phoebe could picture Rose sitting on the stool in her kitchen twirling the phone cord around her finger.

"What's Mom doing for money?"

"She picked up another cleaning job. I got a part-time gig at a restaurant downtown across from the office. We're getting by."

Phoebe drummed her fingers on the shelf under the phone. "I promise you, the second I graduate, every cent I have is going to pay off that medical debt."

"You focus on your thesis and graduation. We've got this for now," Rose promised her.

Phoebe would. And she'd do whatever it took to graduate on time and start supporting her family the way they'd supported her. "It just sucks that you had to get a second job."

She could hear Rose's shrug. "Eh, it's not so bad. Keeps me from having to move back in with Mom and Dad, *and* I met a guy at the restaurant."

Phoebe perked up. Rose was famously picky when it came to men. "What's his name? How did you meet him? What's he like?"

"Is this how you're interrogating your farmer because I think you're doing it wrong," Rose quipped.

"Ugh. Just tell me about the guy."

"His name is Melvin, and he's an auditor. And I don't want to say any more and jinx it, so I'm changing the subject. Have you broken the news to Mom and Dad that you're staying with a hot single man all by your virginal self this summer?"

"First off, I'm no more a virgin than you are, and secondly, God, no! They'd have had a cow and never would have let me if they'd known."

"Where do they think you are?"

"I'm on a *family* farm," Phoebe insisted. The crux of her lie relied on not expanding on how large or small that family was. "Technically it's their fault for not asking more questions."

"Yeah, let me know how that defense holds up," Rose snorted.

"How is the subject ever going to come up unless my smartass sister starts making comments?"

"You keep your mouth shut about Melvin, and I'll keep mine shut about your summer of debauchery."

"There's no debauching going on," Phoebe insisted. She'd made the mistake of mentioning John's ridiculous physical appeal in the letter she'd sent describing her summer plans. "He's gorgeous and sexy and manly, but his personality—or more specifically the distinct lack thereof—is a Big. Fat. Nope."

Rose sighed into the phone. "That's a shame. Your summer would be a lot more fun with some action with hot farmer."

"Yeah, well it would be a lot more *productive* if hot farmer was capable of more than one or two syllables at a time."

"Crap," Rose announced. "I gotta go. I have a perm appointment. Talk in a couple days?"

"Yeah. I miss you, Ro. And I promise as soon as I graduate, I'm taking the burden off you."

"We're family. It's what we do," Rose said. "Go wear down your farmer."

"Go perm your hair."

Phoebe hung up, feeling a mix of determination and dread. She wouldn't let her family down, and she wouldn't let a stubborn, jerky farmer stand in her way either. She just needed a plan. She looked around the square, returning the friendly wave of a family of four wandering the downtown with ice cream cones. The two little girls wore matching hand-made fringed vests.

Maybe soaking up some of the local culture would give her an idea on how best to crack John Pierce like the idiotic egg he was.

7

He found her, finally. Phoebe was perched on a stool in the record shop, massive headphones covering her ears, grinning across the vinyl stacks at fire chief Michael "If She's Got a Rack, I've Got the Time" Cardona. The look Michael was giving Phoebe said he had all the time in the world. The man was his best friend, but that just meant John knew Michael couldn't be trusted.

She slipped the headphones off laughing. "How have I never heard of 'Baby's Got Her Blue Jeans On'?"

"I heard Mel McDaniel's voice in my head the second I saw you walking down the sidewalk," Michael said with a slick wink.

John had seen enough. He wasn't about to let Phoebe be devoured by the man who had taken two women to his senior prom.

They were still laughing, cozy as can be, as he walked up.

"We need to talk." John had never in his entire life issued those words in that order.

Those wicked green eyes widened in surprise.

"Well if it isn't my old friend John!" Michael's enthusiastic reaction put his back up. His friend was hitting on his charge, the charge he'd chased off not an hour ago with his shitty attitude.

"Cardona," John said coolly.

"It looks like the fun police are here," Michael said in a mock whisper to Phoebe who grinned up at him like he was a fucking comedian.

Phoebe cleared her throat, refusing to look in John's direction. "Thank you for the musical education, Michael." She smiled prettily up at him.

Michael tipped his ball cap that sat on top of unruly blond hair. "The pleasure was all mine."

"Give us a minute?" John asked Phoebe. She gave him a shrug of disinterest before wandering into the Pop section.

John waited until she was engrossed in a dig through the discount bin and gave Michael half a shove. "Leave her alone."

Michael, affable as the day was long, just grinned. "Is she off-limits?"

"Way off-limits," John warned him.

"Off-limits because you're..." Michael prompted him.

"I'm in charge of her while she's here," John said, side-stepping the implication.

"If you're not interested, then I'm not seeing a problem." Michael enjoyed a challenge whether it was poured into a pair of hip-hugging jeans or it had two clenched fists like John did currently.

"I didn't say I wasn't interested."

"That's right. You didn't." Michael grinned.

John thought about decking him and decided he didn't want to deal with the blood and the whining.

Michael held up his hands in surrender. "Gotta say, I'm relieved, man. A guy names his pet cow after his high school girlfriend and his friends are bound to worry a bit."

47

John's muttered curse had Michael throwing his head back and laughing. "Don't worry, dude. I'll spread the word. Phoebe is off-limits, and John Pierce isn't losing his damn mind."

"Thanks, asshole," John muttered.

"See you at the meeting?" Michael asked.

"Yeah, I'll be there."

"You bringing Phoebe?"

Taking a page out of his charge's book, John tossed a middle finger over his shoulder as he stalked away.

Unfazed, Cardona whistled his way out of the store, and John set about making things right with Phoebe. He owed her an apology and an explanation. Neither of which would be easy.

She was listening to another song through headphones nearly the size of her head. The store owner, Linus Fitzsimmons, had given her a lollipop that she was enjoying with her music. She jumped when he laid a hand on her shoulder. With reluctance, Phoebe pulled off the headphones.

"I'm not apologizing," she announced.

He blinked. "Okay."

"Okay." She nodded dismissively and made a move to put the headphones back on. But John yanked the plug out of the machine.

"Not done yet."

"Three one-syllable words in a row. Is this some kind of record?"

He felt the corner of his eye twitch and pressed his fingers to the spot. "You drive me insane."

"Back at you." She crossed her arms, assuming a defensive position.

"I owe you an apology. I haven't been welcoming or friendly or cooperative, and I'm sorry."

She eyed him with suspicion. "I don't want to leave. Not without getting what I came for."

He nodded. "I understand."

"If you want me gone, the only way to accomplish that is to cooperate."

John scratched absently at the base of his neck. "Yeah, I'm starting to get that, too."

"So, you'll cooperate?" One eyebrow arched as if in challenge.

"I'll do my best." It was as close to a promise as he could make.

"What exactly annoys you about me so much?" she asked suddenly.

"A lot of things."

She plucked the lollipop out of her mouth. "Gee, thanks."

"I don't mean it like that. You're not annoying. Well, I mean you *are*. But I just wasn't prepared to have my life interrupted by a woman who..."

"Drives you insane?" she supplied, slipping the candy between her pink lips.

"I like you." He said the words quietly, but she caught them all the same.

She blinked. "I annoy you because you like me?"

Verbalizing was not his strong suit, and his frustration was rising. "You weren't what I was expecting."

"Do you think you're what I was expecting? I thought I'd be spending the summer with some elderly man in coveralls who chewed on straw and said 'yep' a lot."

"At least your expectation wasn't that far off. I have coveralls somewhere."

She gave him the tiniest smile, and the knot that had settled in his gut loosened. "I was expecting some young,

49

eager grad student who I could dump shit jobs on and not worry about." *Not spend hours in bed laying there thinking about.*

"I'm not that different from your expectations," Phoebe argued. "I'm perfectly willing to do shit jobs. I just need you to talk to me."

"You're not hearing what I'm not saying," John sighed.

"What are you not saying?"

"I'm attracted to you, and I don't want to be."

"Ohhhh." She drew the word out, and he saw a mixture of surprise and amusement on her face. "That sounds like a problem."

"I know you're laughing at me," John grumbled.

"Kind of hard not to. There are some men out there who don't mind being attracted to a woman who shows up on their doorstep."

"It's not something I'm willing to act on."

Like a dog with a bone, Phoebe dug in. "Why not? Hypothetically, if we were attracted to each other, what would be wrong with exploring those feelings?"

"Well, first of all, I don't know that you feel the same attraction that I do. Me acting on my attraction without regard for your feelings is disrespectful."

"Let's just clear that matter up right now. I find you attractive as hell, John."

He didn't want his blood to pound through his veins like that in reaction to her confession. Didn't want to feel that quiver of hope that swooped through his gut.

"Physically at least," she clarified. "Your personality has yet to be determined."

Hers had been determined from the first second she opened her mouth, he thought wryly. "We're too different. I don't like loud, opinionated women."

"But you like me."

"We're opposites," he said, grasping desperately for the words that would make her understand, make her shut up and leave it all alone. "You belong to Culture Club, and I haven't been more than one state away from Blue Moon my entire life. You're smart. I didn't go to college. You're funny. I think we can both agree that I'm not. And I'm responsible for you while you're staying with me. I don't want to get distracted from that."

Now she looked genuinely confused. "Culture Club?"

"That shirt you wear. Culture Club."

"'Do you really want to hurt me?'"

John shoved a hand through his hair in frustration. "No. Of course I don't want to hurt you. That's what I'm trying to avoid."

She was shaking her head. "It's a song. By Culture Club, a band."

Great. And now he looked like an idiot. "I'm not great with pop culture," he mumbled.

Phoebe looked at him quietly and then slipped off her stool. She walked down the aisle away from him.

"Phoebe." He followed her between the metal racks and bins of vinyl and cassettes. He wasn't going to give up until this was settled. He'd been an ass before, and now he was fucking up his apology. If he could just write it out, deliver it that way, she'd at least understand.

She plucked a tape out of a bin and slapped it against his chest. "Consider it stage one of educating John."

Culture Club *Kissing to Be Clever*.

"If I promise to listen to this and answer fifty percent of your incessant questions, can we start over?"

She gave him a smile that had his blood stirring. "I'd like that."

8

They walked along Main Street, John carrying the bag with his new cassette and Phoebe enjoying the colorful cacophony of storefronts. He sprung for ice cream for dinner at a kitschy little shop called Karma Kustard, and Phoebe considered John fully forgiven.

She'd decided "when in Rome" and went for the Technicolor rainbow cone. John had—predictably—stuck with plain old vanilla.

He seemed to be amused by her reaction to the entire town.

"I just can't believe this place is real." She shook her head, scanning the Frisbee tournament happening in the park across the street.

"What's so unreal about it?"

She rolled her eyes. "Everything. You've lived here your whole life, so you don't even see the fleet of VW vans or the tie-dye twins named Daisy and Dharma who say 'groovy' and 'far out'."

"That's just surface weird. We're pretty normal underneath it all."

"Oh, really? Didn't one of your normal townsfolk con you into believing I was a man?"

"That probably happens everywhere."

She snorted. "When's the last time you left the county? There's a whole wide world of people who mind their own business out there."

John remained silent, content to focus on his ice cream cone.

"Why did she do it, anyway?" Phoebe asked. "What did this Mrs. Normandon—"

"Nordemann," he corrected.

"Nordemann. What did she hope to get out of this? It seems odd for a stranger to be so invested in helping me finish my thesis."

He hemmed and hawed his way to a half-ass answer. "Who knows the workings of the female mind?"

"Me. I do." She drilled her finger into his shoulder. "I know the workings of the female mind. And I know there must have been some kind of reason for her to foist a female grad student on you."

He cleared his throat and took a breath. "Well, then. I expect she wants me to marry you and live happily ever after."

Phoebe's ice cream cone fell out of her hand and splatted on the sidewalk in a puddle of rainbow. "Marry you? She never even met me! I could have been some college coed psychopath! She wouldn't even know if we were compatible. You can't just force two people together and expect them to *get married!* I thought this town was trapped in the '60s not the 1860s."

"Next you're going to tell me that's something that only happens in Blue Moon." John handed her a fistful of napkins

"Yes! It *is*." She stooped to scoop up her sidewalk dessert with a napkin and deposited it in the trashcan. She frowned at him until he offered her his cone. She took a lick, noting the sharpening in his eyes.

"What are you going to do about it?" she asked.

He shrugged, unconcerned. "What can I do?"

"You can't make me marry you."

He laughed. "I have no intention of marrying you. I do have every intention of minding my own business and getting my farm up and running. I have no room for anything else."

They started walking again. "I still think it's weird," Phoebe grumbled.

"Yeah, well, it won't be the weirdest thing you witness here," he predicted.

They walked on in silence passing storefronts—Phoebe wondering how such an insane little town could exist—until she spotted the florist shop. Phoebe paused to study the riotous display of flowers in the window.

"Sunflowers are my favorite," she sighed. "They should be ugly because they're so different, so weird, but instead they're just so happy. How can anyone not think they're beautiful?"

Not expecting an answer, she was surprised when John opened his mouth. "Don't you think that's their appeal? They *are* so different, proud about it, too. Why wouldn't we like them?"

Well, the farmer had some depth to him.

"So, what's the story with you and Michael?" she asked, pulling his cone toward her to catch the vanilla drip with her tongue.

A cloud passed over his face. He closed his eyes. "Why do you have *so many questions*? Jesus, it's like a walking interrogation."

"I'm just curious. I'm not like taking notes and keeping a dossier on you."

"We're friends. Cardona and I grew up together."

"You didn't look very friendly in the store," she countered.

"I didn't like him hitting on you."

Phoebe raised her eyebrows, but before she could jump on him with a dozen questions, John knocked her shoulder companionably. "Shut up."

"There's no way I'm shutting up on that one," she warned him.

"I had a feeling."

"So, you're attracted to me. I'm attracted to you. But you're still not going to act on it because of some sense of responsibility for my well-being, but you also don't want me attracting anyone else," she recounted.

"Exactly," he said, sounding relieved.

She laughed. "You're an odd kind of guy, John Pierce."

"I like to think I'm a sunflower."

She choked. "A legitimate joke *and* an apology from you in the same day? I think I need to sit down."

"I have just the place for you to recuperate." John nudged her toward the movie theater.

"What's Town Meeting?" she asked, reading the marquis.

"It's not a movie. There's a town meeting tonight. I have to go, but you're welcome to join me."

"Yes!" Bouncing on her toes, she barely let him get the words out. "I want to meet everyone here and see you all in action together. It's like getting into a secret society! How many people will be there tonight? Can I ask questions? What's the age range of residents who attend town meetings?"

"You have a curious mind."

"Sociology minor," she explained. "People fascinate me." They moved out of the way of a young couple decked out as if they were from competing decades. She wore her bangs in two-stories high Aqua Net glory, acting as a frame to her turquoise eyeshadow. Her pink satin dress looked like something Molly Ringwald would party in. Her partner was a skinny man in a Jerry Garcia t-shirt that was two sizes too small. His jeans rode low on his nonexistent hips and flared out over platform boots. His curly hair was somewhat tamed under a bandana.

"Hi, John." The girl waved a friendly greeting, cracking her bubble gum.

"Peace, man," the guy said, flashing two fingers.

"Hey Rainbow, Gordon." John nodded. They parted as the '80s and '60s walked between them holding hands.

"What. Was. That?" Phoebe breathed.

"Rainbow Gilbenthal and Gordon Berkowicz. They're an item."

Phoebe grinned. "You're an old soul, John."

He winced. "It's because I said 'an item' isn't it?"

"That and about a thousand other things."

"Does it bother you?"

"I think I kinda like it," she confessed. "Except the part where you think that because I'm a woman I can't do shit jobs."

"It's hard to think about *you* as a farm hand. Not women in general. You specifically."

"I'm not sure if that's better or worse," she admitted.

He settled her in an aisle seat in the theater that had retained its art deco glory. Two seats over, a girl with a chaotic headful of tight black curls grinned at them.

"Stay here and behave, please," John said quietly.

"Aren't you sitting here?" Phoebe asked. She'd hoped that sitting quietly next to him at the little town meeting would give her some time to think. He'd dumped an awful lot on her in a short period of time. From an apology to his admission of attraction, their entire relationship may have just shifted. And Phoebe wanted to know what that meant.

John shook his head, looking a little green around the gills.

"He's gotta participate," the girl with the curls said, tilting her bag of popcorn toward the stage. "Good luck up there, Pierce."

John looked like he was going to toss his ice cream, and Phoebe leaned away just in case.

"I'll meet you after," he said and trudged toward the stairs on the side of the stage like a man facing his death sentence. Phoebe watched him cross the stage and take a seat between two more residents. He pulled a piece of yellow legal paper out of his back pocket and began studying it.

"Elvira Eustace," the woman said, leaning across the empty seat and offering her non-butter-covered hand for a shake.

"Phoebe Allen."

"Oh, you must be John's grad student." Elvira offered the popcorn to Phoebe.

Phoebe dug out a handful of greasy goodness. "I am but not the one he was expecting."

"Mmm, I heard Mrs. Nordemann pulled a fast one on him."

"Yeah, what exactly happened with that? She was my second cousin's college roommate, and when I was looking for a farm to spend the summer on, my aunt said that John and Blue Moon would love to have me."

Elvira chuckled. "Jillian abhors loneliness. She's been happily married since she was nineteen and thinks everyone else should be, too. She figured John out there all by his lonesome on those two hundred acres needed some company."

"Some female company?"

Elvira nodded sagely. "Yep. And she knew he wouldn't 'go gentle into that good night.'"

"So, she pulled a fast one on him."

"There's a lot of fast ones pulled around here. It's part of our charm," Elvira insisted.

"Can you give me a crash course in Blue Moon?" Phoebe begged.

"First, you shouldn't have left a seat between us. Blue Moon is all about acceptance and snooping in other people's business, and that means giving up all rights to your personal space."

Eagerly, Phoebe slid over a seat and Elvira laughed. "Next lesson, young grasshopper, always expect the unexpected."

The lights dimmed, and the milling crowd took their seats, quieting down to a dull roar. A woman in jeans with a gun strapped to her belt strode across the stage to the podium.

"Who's that?" Phoebe whispered.

"That's Sheriff Hazel Garfunkle. She'll run the meeting tonight. Mayor Nordemann—your matchmaker's husband—is down with bronchitis according to Gordon Berkowicz and a broken ankle according to Farmer Carson. Bruce Oakleigh insists it's a fishing trip."

Hazel shook hands with the residents on stage and then settled in to start the meeting. She leaned on the podium with the ease of a lifetime resident surrounded by friends and spoke into the microphone. "Yeah, okay. Let's get this meeting started so we can all get home. I've been asked to remind everyone that, as close as we all are, it's still illegal to push your face up against your neighbor's windows and look inside."

Phoebe snickered, convinced it was a joke, and then silenced herself when hands shot up everywhere in the audience.

"Is this serious?" she hissed at Elvira.

"Oh, yeah. We had an incident last week where a certain busybody got worried that she hadn't seen the Guzmans outside the house in a while. This is after she read an article in the paper about a carbon monoxide leak that killed four in Iowa. So, she sneaks over in her house dress and peeps in the window on the front porch."

"What did she see?"

"The Guzmans having sex on the living room rug. At least that's what they were doing until they saw her plastered up against their window gaping at them."

Phoebe's laugh escaped as a raspberry against her palm. The woman in front of her turned around and frowned at her. "Sorry," Phoebe whispered.

"A lot more questions than I was thinking there'd be for a pretty straightforward ordinance," Hazel sighed. "All right, we'll start with you, Clayton."

A large man with an even larger afro and white silk shirt unfolded himself from his seat. "Thanks, Sheriff. I was just wondering like what if you see smoke coming from inside the house?"

Hazel was obviously a pro at handling Blue Mooners. "In that case, I think it's safe to look and make sure no one's inside."

Appeased, Clayton nodded and sat back down. More hands shot up.

"Tuesday," Hazel pointed at a woman wearing a tie-dye leotard over black tights.

"Her name's Tuesday, and she teaches at the aerobics studio," Elvira said before Phoebe could even ask.

"Yeah, like what if we don't see smoke but we hear something?" Tuesday twirled the crimped end of her ponytail around her finger.

"Can you give us an example?" Hazel asked.

Tuesday let out a blood-curdling scream that silenced the theater. Phoebe clutched a hand to her chest.

"Right. Okay. A scream like that, I'd start knocking on the front door, and if no one answered, go ahead and look in the windows. Just be sure it's not the Fitzsimmons kid because he's got a crazy set of lungs on him and makes everything sound like bloody murder."

"Thanks, sheriff," Tuesday said cheerfully and bopped back into her seat.

A dozen more hands raised.

9

"*O*kay, so I think we've gotten this as fleshed out as we're able to," Hazel announced. "No peeping unless the house is on fire, someone's screaming bloody murder, a vehicle has veered off the road and driven into the residence, you witness suspicious activity such as someone else peeping in the windows and then disappearing, and/or you have express permission from the police department or other community leader including but not limited to myself, the fire chief, and the mayor."

She looked out over the audience, and Phoebe sent up a little prayer that no one else had an amendment. It had taken them half an hour to get through all the "what-ifs."

Hazel picked up the gavel and whacked it. "Moving on. We've got a few citizens who are gonna talk about some stuff. So, give 'em your ears."

First up was Sylvia Needleman, dressed in head-to-toe black, who wanted to educate Blue Moon on the dangers of microwaving food. Her shy librarian demeanor completely transformed when she spoke about radiation waves and TV dinners.

Next up was a burly guy in chinos named Bruce who, for a young preppie, was unusually passionate about history. He was trying to drum up votes for an authentic 4th of July celebration with a recreation of the signing of the Declaration of Independence.

When it was John's turn to take the podium, Phoebe sat a little straighter. She was curious what a man of few words would have to say to an entire community. He looked out into the audience and pulled out his piece of notebook paper.

Someone slid into the empty seat on her right, and Phoebe glanced over into Michael Cardona's mischievous eyes. "What did I miss?" he asked, reaching over her for Elvira's popcorn.

"Thirty minutes on reasons why you should peep in your neighbor's windows," Elvira whispered. "What are you doing here?"

"Messing with John," Michael said, throwing an arm around the back of Phoebe's seat and spreading out in all directions.

Elvira rolled her eyes. "Men are basically children," she sighed.

Phoebe nodded in agreement until John's gaze tracked to her. She saw the narrowing of his eyes, and Michael's corresponding shit-eating grin.

John gave Michael a good hard glare before clearing his throat. The mic picked up something that sounded pretty close to "asshole." Michael snickered but dropped his arm from Phoebe's shoulders.

John smoothed a hand over his paper and began to read. "As you know, I reluctantly represent Blue Moon's farming community thanks to a vote that occurred when I wasn't present." The audience chuckled.

"In that capacity, I've had the opportunity to discuss some of the pressing matters our farmers face. We can narrow the biggest of them down to two issues: a lack of equipment and a lack of labor. Some of our farms have the equipment necessary but lack the hands to help. Others lack the equipment but have the labor."

Phoebe listened raptly and noted that the audience was doing the same. It seemed that on the rare occasion when John Pierce spoke his mind, people listened.

"Our community is unique in many aspects, the best of them being our ability and desire to come together as a whole to support those who need it. We share what's ours just as naturally as we gossip and snoop."

Again, the audience tittered. Blue Moon apparently had a healthy sense of humor about its own quirks.

"Keeping that in mind, I have a proposal for the farmers of Blue Moon. By working as a team, a family—something we do quite naturally already—we could share access to top-of-the-line equipment and available labor, finishing work faster and more efficiently than if we keep our resources to ourselves."

Hands began to fly up around the theater.

"Now, hang on. Let me get the rest of this out. If I lose my place now, I'll never find my way back."

Good-naturedly, the hands were withdrawn. *Who knew community leadership could be sexy?* Phoebe mused.

"Let me give you an example of how I foresee this working. Carson's down a foreman this season, but he does have a semi for hauling grain. Now when Carson isn't using that truck, it's sitting there costing money, requiring maintenance. But if he would rent it out to the rest of us—for a reasonable fee—he'd have a nice little income that covers the cost of gas and maintenance. Or instead of cash, we could arrange a labor/equipment swap. I'd give him X amount of hours on his farm in return for use of the truck."

The hands were back up, but John plowed on, his eyes glued to his speech, determined to get to the end.

"Another option would be renting equipment from the farm supply in Cleary. A couple of us have combines, but none of us have access to the newer technology which significantly cuts harvest time. If we pool our resources for say a four or five-day rental, the rental costs would be negligible, and the work would get done faster than if we tackled harvest on our own."

Phoebe leaned in to Elvira. "It sounds like a great idea, but isn't that kind of like communism?" she whispered.

Elvira laughed softly. "We prefer to think of it as commune-ism."

After revisiting the broader points of unity and sharing, John's speech stalled out, and Phoebe bet money he hadn't written a conclusion. She bit her lip when he let out a long "Soooooo..."

Hazel moved up on John's elbow and leaned into the mic. "So, anyone interested in John's farm-sharing concept— which, if you want my two cents, is a smart idea—should reach out directly to John. I think we've covered everything we need to tonight so let's adjourn."

Hazel was smart enough not to let anyone else make a motion or ask one last question. She banged the gavel and hauled ass off the stage.

"All business that one," Michael said, glaring in Hazel's direction.

"You've just got your Fruit of the Looms in a bunch because Hazel turned you down for prom," Elvira said, crumpling up her empty popcorn bag.

"You asked her to prom?" Phoebe asked, jumping on what had to be a good story.

Michael sulked and shrugged one shoulder. "I wasn't serious."

"Oh, I call bullshit!" Elvira pointed a dagger-like fingernail in his direction. "If you were just kidding, you wouldn't have taken two Playboy wannabees in her place."

"You took two women to your prom to spite the sheriff?"

"She wasn't sheriff at the time," Michael argued.

"Cardona here hasn't learned that if he keeps playing games with the ladies, he's going to get burned," Elvira predicted.

"I'm the fire chief. I think I can handle the heat." Michael gave Phoebe an exaggerated wink.

JOHN WISHED he could just part the crowds like a tight end and drag Phoebe out of here. He hadn't been expecting such an enthusiastic reception to his idea, had actually thought there was a good possibility it would flop. But the dozen farmers standing between him and beating the hell out of Cardona seemed to really like the idea.

He tried to focus on what Old Man Carson was saying, but his attention kept getting dragged back to Phoebe laughing up into Cardona's asshole face. The guy was probably charming the hell out of her and he couldn't do a damn thing about it. His friend never knew when to quit with a joke.

Ernest Washington, one of Carson's friends since birth laid a hand on John's arm. "How about we all get together out at John's later this week to discuss? Sunday work for everyone?" There were nods and "yeps" around the circle surrounding them. "Good. See you all Sunday at 3. Bring beer."

The crowd dispersed, and John turned to Ernest. "Thank you."

"Don't waste time thanking me. Go get your girl away from Prince Charming before he casts his spell on her."

John didn't bother arguing that Phoebe wasn't his girl. He dove into the milling crowd and waded his way toward her. Town meetings always took forever because once Blue Moon got to talking, it was impossible to shut them up. He didn't blame Mayor Nordemann for skipping out on this one on account of his eczema acting up.

He side-stepped a heated conversation about TV dinners between the town librarian Sylvia and Mrs. McCafferty from the farm store. He was within feet now, and his fingers flexed with the desire to drag Michael out of his seat and throw him down in the aisle. He'd warned him, hadn't he?

But his chances at a surprise attack were decimated when Jillian Nordemann jumped in front of him. "There's our farm hero," she chirped, hands clasped under her chin. "Tell me everything. How's life on the farm with Phoebe?"

John's anger was temporarily deflected onto the new target. "Jillian. Why did you tell me Phoebe was a man?"

Jillian's cat-that-ate-the-canary expression told him it hadn't been an accident. "Why, that's ridiculous! Why wouldn't I have told you Phoebe was a woman?"

"I haven't the slightest idea. That's why I'm asking," he said flatly.

She brought a finger to her chin and tapped it. "I assure you I never meant to mislead you."

Jillian Nordemann was a bald-faced liar.

"Actually. Now that I think about it, I'm sure this mix up is all your fault. Why on earth would you think a man was named Phoebe?"

"You didn't tell me his... her name was Phoebe. You said Allen."

"Phoebe Allen," Jillian nodded, pleased. "That's her name."

"You left out the Phoebe part," he growled.

"Oh, my! Did I? How silly of me." She fanned her face. "Are you quite sure? That doesn't sound like something I would forget."

The ditz card had never been particularly successful with John, and Jillian's version was only giving him a headache.

"Are you sure I never mentioned Phoebe was a woman? Well, what exactly did you expect when I said Phoebe?"

"You *didn't say* Phoebe. You *said* Allen!" Ditzy and deaf were not endearing traits to John.

"Have you had that eye twitch looked at?" Jillian wondered, prodding him just under his right eye.

"I didn't have it until Phoebe showed up when I was expecting Allen." He was almost shouting now, and it still had no effect on the woman.

"Well, I'm glad it all worked out for the best," she said, waving away his complaint. "It's very important for her to graduate, and soon, you know. Especially since her father was in that dreadful accident. And her mother has never worked outside the home. Poor things are just drowning in debt. There just isn't enough money at home for another semester let alone all those medical bills. You're really doing her a wonderful favor by letting her stay the summer."

John's mouth opened and then closed again without any words escaping.

"Oh! There's Mrs. Beezerman. I need to go ask her about Bunco Friday night. Excuse me." She dashed off into the fray before John could explain to her what an injustice she'd done to him or grill her about Phoebe's family.

John decided giving chase wouldn't give him any satisfaction. What would was making Cardona think he was going to pound his face in.

He had two rows of seats to go when Michael spotted him. His friend's feet hit the floor, and he was already out of his seat as he tossed a friendly, "Gotta go!" to Phoebe and Elvira. Michael vaulted over the two empty rows behind them before veering into the aisle and sprinting out of the building.

Phoebe watched him go. "You two have the oddest friendship."

They bid Elvira goodbye but not before Phoebe exchanged phone numbers with her. "I could use someone with lady parts to hang out with on occasion," Phoebe joked.

"Count on me. And I'll be on the farm Sunday for the party."

"Party?" John looked at her blankly.

"Yeah, the farmers and everyone are coming over to talk about the farm sharing?" Elvira prompted him.

"That happened seven seconds ago, and it was just a couple of farmers coming over for a meeting," John argued.

Elvira gave a dainty shrug. "Not what I heard. You better stock up on picnic food and beer. It'll be a prequel to the festivities on the 4th."

John watched her go with a sinking feeling of dread in the pit of his stomach. And here he'd thought the speech would be the worst part.

Phoebe patted John on the shoulder. "You okay?"

He shook his head. "I just want a cold beer and my nice quiet house and to never see any of these crazies again."

"Come on, let's go home and get you that beer," she said, leading him up the aisle. "You know. This is why people own TVs."

10

*N*eeding a little distance from Phoebe, John strapped a spray tank of weed killer on her back and sent her off to trudge the perimeter of the wheat fields. She'd cheerfully skipped off for the fields, whistling some pop song that he should know but didn't, leaving him broody.

Last night had opened a door. One that he hadn't been prepared to open. One that he needed to close again. Yes, he was attracted to her. Yes, she interested him beyond just house guest status. But attraction and interest? Those didn't outweigh responsibility and plans.

He'd been surprised by his uncomfortable, visceral reaction to Michael flirting with Phoebe. Sure, he was responsible for her while she was here, but that reaction had bordered on territorial. He didn't need the distraction of attraction stirring him up every five seconds.

She'd dressed in a tight t-shirt today that he'd immediately noticed and appreciated on an uncontrollable biological level. Her jeans had more rips than denim, and she'd borrowed one of his ball caps from the coat closet and fed her hair through the back in a long tail. And all he could think about was how pretty she looked. Then she'd smiled at him, and she was beautiful.

Fortunately, she'd immediately peppered him with questions about his pull-behind sprayer, its age and dimensions, and whether or not he reckoned it would last one more season. The yammering demands for information made the beauty a little easier to ignore.

The woman had him tied up in knots one minute with her incessant interrogation and then left him smiling like a dope after her as she sauntered out of the room tossing insults at him. She hadn't oversold her energy or commitment to work. He knew that now and was grateful, even if it did unnerve him. Hell, everything about her unnerved him, including how much he wanted her. His attraction to her was a complication, and John hated those.

Phoebe Allen was the walking contradiction of everything he thought he'd wanted in a woman. Opinionated, aggressive, pushy, headstrong. She made snap decisions, and she never shut up. But here he was, up to his elbows in grease trying to coax the ancient sprayer into operation for one more season, and his thoughts were on her.

He plotted through his options in his mind as he liked to do when faced with a decision.

As far as he saw it, he had two choices. He could pursue some kind of summer fling with her, or he could stay the course, maintain a professional relationship with her, and wait out the summer. Or, they could defy the odds, fall in love, get married, and live happily ever after. *Okay, three choices.*

He smirked at the ludicrous idea, twisting the reassembled nozzle back into place on the boom of the sprayer and moved on to the next one. He'd taken them apart, cleaned them, fixed what was broken, and was now reassembling the whole, hoping it would perform as good as, if not better than, before.

That's how he worked. That's how he lived. He didn't make snap decisions—with the exception of being conned into taking on a grad student. He figured out how things worked and then carefully maintained, tweaked, and finessed until he was satisfied. It was part of the appeal of farm life. Something always needed fixing, there was always a better way to do things, and there was always a simple way to measure success.

Phoebe operated on a manual he didn't have access to, and there'd be no fixing her rashness, her loud opinions. Polar opposites did not make solid marriage material. He was a "stop and smell the bee balm" kind of man. Phoebe was a "blindly stomp all over the bee balm while listing six different ways to make it grow better" person.

John tightened the bolts on the boom and moved on to inspect the hoses.

He was a man that committed whether it was to a task, a woman, a livelihood. He didn't take relationships lightly. Loyalty, to him, was the most valuable component in a relationship. And an affair with Phoebe while exciting and fun— he shook his head to ward off the half dozen visions of her naked and gasping his name—was still ill-conceived. There was no long-term to be had there. Not even if they magically became more compatible.

Phoebe was here for school, not sex. And at the end of the summer, she'd be off to take some fancy job out of some fancy city—that he'd likely never visited—to buckle down and take care of her family. From the gossip Mrs. Nordemann had dumped on him, it sounded as though Phoebe needed cash and a lot of it. She couldn't make that kind of money here. *He* couldn't provide that kind of money for her.

They couldn't make a go of it long-term, and he knew that.

And without that potential for long-term... well he was no Michael Cardona. Sex was more than a hobby to John, and he had to care for his partner. *Sex.* An image of Phoebe, lips parted, eyes heavy-lidded, bloomed in his mind. Her breath warm on his face, her body soft and pliable under his.

His dick stirred, making known its contempt of the recent dry spell. John's grip on the wrench slipped and he rapped his knuckles hard against gritty metal. "Get it together, you fucking idiot," he muttered to himself, shaking out his bloody hand. He looked for a rag to clean up the blood and finding none, shucked off his t-shirt to use as temporary first aid.

The stinging of his knuckles firmed up his decision, and John considered the debate settled. There would be no fling, no affair, just two adults sharing a kitchen table. They could be professional, maybe even tentative friends. In fact, if he got to know her a little better, he imagined their differences would build a bigger gap between them. That would help his physical reaction to her.

Keep things simple, uncomplicated. Just the way he liked them.

Bolstered by that thought, he went back to work whistling.

HE WAS STILL SWEATING and swearing over the sprayer when Phoebe bopped back into the barn with an empty spray tank.

She tossed out a snappy salute. "Private Allen reporting for duty."

He turned her way, and her eyes widened as they zeroed in on his shirt.

"What the hell did you do to yourself?" she demanded, rushing over with the tank bouncing wildly on her back.

She was pawing at his shirt trying to pull it up. Her frantic touch was doing nothing to cool his overheated blood that was once again plunging south. He slapped her hands away and pushed her back a step. Manhandling him was not helping him convince his body that it was best to leave her the hell alone.

"I'm fine." He held up his hand with the sloppy bandage on his knuckles.

"Geez, I thought you punctured something and were oozing liver blood," Phoebe sighed out in relief.

He wasn't quite ready to forgive her for occupying so many of his thoughts this morning and responded with a noncommittal grunt.

"Did you get the old girl working?" Phoebe asked, patting the sprayer.

"Looks that way. You finish the wheat?" He wiped his hands clean on a fresh rag and helped her out of the tank's harness, careful not to let his hands linger.

"Boundaries have been officially eradicated of weeds," she reported. "By the way, what is in that spray? It smells like flowers and garbage."

"It's a special Blue Moon blend weed killer. We try to keep the chemical use low for both cost and potential environmental impact. It works. Not as well as some of the commercial weed killers. But enough that we can justify continuing to use it."

"Good answer," she said, rewarding him with a wink. "Does any farm in Blue Moon use commercial weed killer?" Phoebe asked, slipping into interrogation mode.

John pulled up the hem of his t-shirt and used it to mop his forehead. "We Blue Moon farmers are a little skeptical of the miracles of modern chemistry," he admitted. "It just seems like meddling with Mother Nature isn't the best idea."

Phoebe frowned like she was committing his words to memory. "Interesting. What about technology? For instance, you've got a small, ancient sprayer here. If you were to upgrade to the twenty-foot boom sprayer you'd cut down on your labor hours for production."

"Chicken. Egg," John said. "New equipment requires income. In order for a farmer to have an income, he—or she —" he said, eyeing her up. "Must have a product to sell."

"Mmm, I get it. So, you chose to use available, albeit elderly, equipment rather than going into debt to acquire newer equipment. Valuing your money over your time, essentially."

"Yeah. Can we talk about this later?" John grumbled.

"Sure," Phoebe chirped. "What's next?"

"Next I have to split myself in two so I can spray the corn fields today and haul the rest of the grain to the elevator in Cleary."

"The curse of never enough time," she said with sympathy. "You can't hire more hands until you've made some money, and you can't make any money without a harvest."

"Bingo."

"I'll spray," Phoebe volunteered.

"Phoebe, you want me to turn you loose on my fields in a piece of equipment that's nearly as old as you are?" His tone made it clear that he couldn't think of a worse idea.

"Why don't you show me how it's done and let me take a test pass or two on the field. Ride along, and if you're satisfied I'm not going to mow over your entire crop, you haul the grain."

"And if I'm not satisfied?"

"Oh, you will be, John," she predicted with a wicked grin.

"YOU'VE DONE THIS BEFORE," he shouted his accusation in her ear over the drone of the tractor's engine as they bumped through the field. She was on her third pass, expertly cutting the turns and maintaining a straight line through the furrows. He was wedged in behind her, leaning against the wheel well, his leg hooked over the seat behind her.

He was trying hard not to notice that her head was at crotch height and if she turned—and he sucked at not noticing.

"Didn't I mention that I did this on my grandfather's farm for four or five years before they sold it?" she yelled back, grinning.

"No, you did not mention that, smartass."

"I think you can go deliver your grain. I've got this," she said, cutting the engine as they emerged from the field. "Might want to change your shirt first though. You look like you got stabbed."

He stared down at her and then back at his beloved corn. "Don't stray from the furrows. Keep an eye on the spray. If you notice anything wonky, it's probably a pinched hose. Unkink it and give it a few whacks. Don't swerve, don't get stuck, don't—"

"I got it. You can trust me. I promise not to destroy your crop, okay?"

Reluctantly, he slid out from behind her and stepped down off the ancient tractor. He didn't want to have to trust her. He didn't want to depend on Phoebe to help him get his work done. Didn't want to depend on anyone really. This was *his* livelihood. To her it was just a summer assignment.

"I can just run the grain tomorrow and take care of the fields today. Or maybe I can run it today, and if there's time left this afternoon, I can start the fields—"

"Relax, John. It's going to be fine." And before he could look for another out, another reason not to trust her with this task, she started the tractor and turned into the field.

He watched for another minute trying to calculate her speed so he could flag her down if she was going too fast or too slow. The groundspeed had to be just right or the nozzles needed to be recalibrated. He watched in vain hoping for a mistake that would require correction and further supervision, but she made none.

On an oath, he turned his back on his precious fields and stalked toward the barn praying that he'd return to an intact crop.

PHOEBE GRINNED over her victory when she saw John's figure recede from the tractor's rear-view mirror.

Was there anything more satisfying than surprising someone who doubted you? She couldn't think of one.

She'd thought John would have put up a tougher fight, but she'd played the right cards. His time was valuable *and* limited. By taking a low-skill labor task away from him, he could focus his time on more important things. And, if she didn't royally fuck it up, she'd win some points from John.

She cared what he thought of her. He was good at what he did, smart, and dedicated. Those traits pushed the right buttons with her. So, he wasn't funny, and he knew absolutely nothing about what was popular on TV or the radio these days. She could overlook that.

What had pushed her past interested and into intrigued was watching John in action, poetically explaining the plight of Blue Moon's farmers. It had been a delicious peek into what went on beneath his superior surface. They were still testing each other out, she thought, making another swinging turn with the tractor. But so far, she liked what she saw in him. *A lot.*

And she had to admit that his confession of attraction hadn't been far from her mind since she'd heard it. She'd only taken it out to admire or mull over every hour or so. She'd certainly felt it when their hands brushed and in the way he looked at her when Michael had flirted harmlessly with her. Phoebe liked the zing that shot up her spine when John looked at her with those gray eyes that were anything but cool.

She liked sex but was choosy about her partners. And there was something about John that made her want to shuck her jeans and throw her naked self at him. A clear green light was essential in a healthy sexual relationship, and she had a feeling John wouldn't act on his baser instincts without one.

The thought of it gave her goosebumps now under the early summer sun.

John Pierce was a challenge on every level. He hadn't wanted her here in the first place, and now she could only assume that he'd spend the rest of their time together avoiding his confessed attraction for whatever reasons he conjured in his mind. But there was something John didn't know about her. Phoebe lived for a good challenge. There was nothing more satisfying than sitting down at the end of the day with dragons slayed, mountains climbed, and detours conquered.

And right now, she was eyeing him up as a very enjoyable conquest.

She peeked over her shoulder again and noticed the two nozzles on the far left had shut off their spray.

Yep. Nothing like a good challenge to get the blood moving.

---

11

*P*hoebe rolled her shoulders back to ease the soreness and lifted her face to the breeze. The screen door opened behind her, and a beer floated in front of her face. She grinned up at John the Beer Fairy.

"Thanks," she said, accepting the bottle and giving him her brightest smile. He gave her a long hard look and backed up a pace.

She'd heard the truck in the driveway while popping the roast in the oven and had watched from the window as John walked up the path behind the barn to see if she was still working.

"You, uh, get the fields done?" he asked casually.

Phoebe hid her smile. "Yep."

"I didn't see the sprayer out," he ventured.

He was cute when he was nervous. "I parked it back in the barn. Had to do a little rigging with the hoses."

John was off the porch like a horse out of the gate, and Phoebe tagged along behind him as he headed for the barn. She could read him like the Sunday comics, knowing he was mulling over the thousand ways he assumed she'd ruined his life.

She gave him a minute alone in the barn before ambling in and plopping down on a three-legged stool inside the door.

He turned to look at her and then went back to studying her work on the sprayer.

The second time he turned around to stare at her, she took pity on him. Phoebe slid off the stool and crossed to him. She pointed out the hose configuration on each end of the tank. "The hoses kink between the boom and the tank on the turns. It's a design flaw. So, with a little creative engineering and sturdy tape, I repositioned them."

He looked baffled and just a little impressed, which had Phoebe's toes curling with pleasure inside her boots.

"Not bad," he said, finally.

The minimal praise felt satisfying. *Better than any A on any paper*, Phoebe thought, her smile smug. She strutted back to the doorway and leaned against the frame.

"Oh, and I started a grocery list for the party Sunday, dinner's in the oven—pot roast—and Murdock ran through what looks like an entire field of burrs, but I picked them off him and gave him a bath." Now she was just bragging, but damn it felt good to prove herself useful. "Everything go okay with the grain?"

John nodded and reluctantly gave up studying her engineering marvel. He joined her, leaning against the opposite side of the opening, thumbs looped in his pockets. "I can't believe I'm saying this, but I couldn't have done it without you."

She fluttered her lashes at him. "There, that wasn't so terrible, was it?"

He nudged her foot with his. It was a playful gesture, but it still fanned sparks inside her.

"Listen," he began.

"Uh-oh."

"Let me say my piece," he insisted.

Phoebe gestured grandly. "You have the podium, sir."

"I think the reason we've had trouble talking is I don't know you very well," John started. He pointed a finger in her face when she opened her mouth. "Shut it. I'm well-aware of whose fault that is. But I think if I get to know you, I'll feel more comfortable talking about what I'm doing here."

She waited until she was sure he was done. "Sounds fair. It's like dating."

He blanched. She grinned.

"It's definitely *not* like dating," he insisted.

Phoebe rolled her eyes. "It's exactly like dating. We need to get to know each other in order to establish a relationship. That's basically what we need to do here."

"Minus the actual dating?" His tone was hopeful, and Phoebe scented the challenge.

"That seems like an early assumption," she shrugged. "As you so astutely pointed out, we don't know each other. I don't think we should jump to any conclusions about dating or not dating until we've gotten to know each other better."

"Are you saying you would consider dating me?" he asked. He looked nervous, now, his tan face losing its color, and the adorable twitch appeared at the corner of his eye.

"Well, I don't know." She tapped a finger to her chin. "We already know that this... *arrangement* is only temporary. And based on your old-fashioned tendencies, I would guess that you aren't open to something like that."

"You think I'm old-fashioned?" John demanded.

"It's a first impression," she said, waving away his bubbling temper. "My dad's the same way. You both open doors, you carry things, you don't think I can pull my own weight—"

"Let's get that one cleared up right now," John said briskly. "Me questioning your ability to help out here has nothing to do with your gender. Many of the men I know wouldn't be helpful out here. It's not necessarily a physical ability. This is hard, back-breaking work with the constant looming possibility that Mother Nature could turn on you and ruin your year. Day in and day out, you have to be strong enough to face that and still keep going, still find an appreciation and a respect for it. And if the physical work isn't enough to be its own reward to someone, then they're not going to last a summer out here let alone a lifetime."

Phoebe picked at the label on her beer and nodded. It was the longest speech he'd ever given her. "I totally get that. Is that what attracted you to farming?"

He shook his head. "Hang on. Before we dig into me, let's talk about you. Tell me about your family."

Phoebe blinked. "My family?" Okay, she hadn't been prepared to shift gears that quickly.

John nodded. "You mentioned your dad."

"Well..." How could she sum up her family and what they meant to her? "My parents are wonderful people. They married right out of high school and are still best friends. My dad is overprotective to the point that he had to be talked out of all-girls private schools for me and my sister. Rose is a year younger than me. She graduated college last year."

"If your dad's so overprotective, why did he agree to let you spend the summer on my farm? Alone."

Oh, boy. Phoebe cleared her throat. For an innocent little lie, it sure came up a lot. "Education is important to my parents. My sister and I were the first Allens to finish college," she said with pride. "My parents know they can trust me."

"And they can trust me to keep our relationship purely

professional," John said with a little too much enthusiasm for Phoebe's liking. "What do your parents do?"

Phoebe hesitated. "My mom is a housewife and volunteered for about a hundred organizations. She just started working outside the home part-time this year. My dad was a lineman for the power company."

"Did he retire?"

She took a deep breath and wrinkled her nose. "I'm not exactly sure how well you want to get to know me," she confessed. "Some of this is a little messy."

John was quiet for a moment. "I'd like to know if you're okay telling me."

She nodded and took a fortifying sip of beer. "Dad had an accident a few months back. He was working on a line, and the lift—in the bucket truck—failed. He fell from twenty feet, and it was touch-and-go for a bit. Really scared us." Her voice quivered.

She cleared her throat. "Sorry," she said. "Still scary to think about it. Mind if we walk and talk? I do better if I'm moving."

John nodded and pushed away from the door.

"He had to have emergency surgery. His leg was badly broken. He's doing a lot better now. He's home and in physical therapy. But the medical bills are astronomical, and he lost his job. The company said he was going to be laid off anyway, but it would be a long, expensive legal battle to prove that they were just trying to wiggle out of financial responsibility."

She kicked at a rock, sending it skittering up the path in front of them.

John remained quiet, but he took her hand and squeezed. He didn't let go. Just walked by her side, his hand covering hers.

"Are you sure you want to hear all this?"

"I am."

Phoebe sighed. "Anyway, that's why my mom started working again, and my sister took a second job. Every spare cent Rose makes goes back to them. Things are tight. Really tight. But as soon as I get this degree and a job, I'm paying off whatever I can for them. They're a month behind on their mortgage already, and I've loved school, but I need to start giving back. They've done so much for me."

She fought back the tears that made her throat burn. John released her hand and just when she thought she'd gone too far with the confession, he slid his arm around her shoulders and tugged her into his side. Her body sang. The casual touch set off a flood of heat in her system, and she glanced up at him to see if he noticed that she was now on fire.

But he kept his gaze locked on the horizon as they walked. "You miss them?" he asked.

She nodded and cleared her throat to loosen the lump. "Yeah. They're pretty much the best people I know, and I feel like I'm costing them more by finishing school instead of dropping out and helping them. I guess that's why I'm coming on so strong. It's not just me and my ambitions. I'm ready to repay them, and I'll be able to do that with this degree and the jobs that open up for me."

His fingers stroked her upper arm.

She blew out a breath. "Bet you're sorry you asked," she joked.

"Why didn't you say all that when you got here?"

"It's not the kind of shit you dump on a complete stranger, John."

"It is in Blue Moon," he argued and looked down at her, and she felt that familiar warmth filling up her belly. He slipped his arm off her shoulder as if he'd just now realized where it was.

"I'm not a Mooner," she reminded him. "Where we come from, your problems are your own, not fodder for a town meeting."

John sighed wistfully. "That sounds nice."

Phoebe laughed. "From the outside, your 'commune-ism' is pretty attractive." She raised her beer to her lips and drank. "It's been a rough patch for my family, but I know there's a light at the end of the tunnel. Once I have a job, my only goal in life is taking care of $20,000 in medical debt."

"Then what?" John asked. "After you take care of that?"

Phoebe blinked. "Oh, the usual. Make a difference, lead a meaningful life, have statues erected to me for my research in the farming industry. You?"

"Make a go of this," he said, jutting his chin toward the barn.

"Yeah? Maybe they'll erect scarecrows to you for being outstanding in your field?" She waited a beat, wondering if the joke would go over his head.

"You're hilarious," he said dryly.

"You know, most people laugh at my humor."

"I'm laughing on the inside. Do you ever think about having a family?" he asked, swiftly changing the subject.

"Sure. If I meet the right guy." She looked down the dirt drive, pastures flowing off to the west in a million shades of green, fields of wheat to the east. "I think I'll have all girls and raise them to believe they can do anything they damn well please."

His grin was quick and warm and made her heart stumble. "If anyone can, it'd be you."

"What about you? Family or the solitude you so love so dearly?"

He squinted out across the low rolling hills. "Definitely family. Someday."

"Boys to help you build the Pierce family farming empire?" Phoebe fished.

"Who says girls wouldn't do just as good a job empire-building?" John teased.

"Why, Mr. Pierce," Phoebe fluttered her eyelashes at him. "Be careful, your tolerance is showing."

He gave her a long, searching look. One that had goose-bumps cropping up on her arms despite the warmth of the sun. "How much time do we have before dinner?" he asked. She took the arm he had looped around her shoulder and looked at his watch. "Another half an hour.

"Come with me," he said.

"Where are we going?"

"I want to show you something."

She took his hand. "Can I take my beer?"

12

They stopped by the house for fresh beers and a peek in the oven. Satisfied that dinner would be perfection, Phoebe followed John out the door again and hoped that he'd put his arm around her again.

He didn't. But he walked close enough that the back of his hand brushed hers in a repeated reminder of his presence and the giddy effect he had on her hormones. They crested the hill behind the house and followed a worn, grassy path that divided pasture and field. To the east, an old stone barn stood dark and tall, dominating the landscape of golds and greens.

"Is that yours, too?" she asked.

John looked up at the barn, squinted. "Yeah. It's got good bones. Someday it'll be something."

He led her to the edge of the cornfield.

"Mind getting a little dirtier?" John asked her.

Phoebe looked down at the jeans she'd worn all day, which had a new hole and a thick layer of dirt and dust. "I think I can handle it."

He gestured toward the fresh turned dirt at the corner of

the field. Stalks of sweet corn poked out of the ground in tidy rows. "Sit."

She sat cross-legged in the dirt and stared at him expectantly. "Now what?"

He sat next to her, their knees touching. "Be quiet. Just be."

She arched an eyebrow at him, but he ignored her and closed his eyes. Skeptical and wondering if this was an elaborate set up for him to smash a clod of dirt in her face, Phoebe closed an eye. It took a minute or two of peeking at him to make sure she wasn't in danger of a dirt strike.

Deciding that whatever he wanted to show her must be important, Phoebe reluctantly let her defenses slip. She willed her mind to quiet, wiping away thoughts like words on a chalkboard, and sat. The sun felt warm on her skin, and she heard the whisper of wind rustling through leaves and the buzz of cicadas and bees. It sounded like a never-ending conversation. The smell of the turned dirt under her was fresh, metallic.

And there it was, that buzz beneath her skin. A vibration of sameness. She felt part of it, part of the earth beneath her that she'd spent her day tending, part of the air that caressed her skin and filled her lungs. She felt John next to her, too. Her senses were keenly aware of his presence as if, somehow, he were the anchor of it all. Rooted and reaching at the same time, Phoebe felt like they were like the green stalks that stretched on beyond them in an organic patchwork.

Their efforts here would never be wasted. What was put into the land would come back. That was the promise.

She let her eyes flutter open and found John watching her, a softness on his face she hadn't seen before. The blue of the sky, the gray of his eyes, the green of the grass. In the silence of her mind, everything was so much more vibrant.

"Find it?" he asked.

She nodded without speaking.

He laughed softly. "This is the first time I've seen you without words," he teased.

"They'll come back, and when they do, you'll regret it," she warned him. But he was still smiling when he opened the cooler. He handed her a fresh beer.

"Okay, I definitely felt it. But you're going to have to explain it to me."

"That's my 'why.' That's why instead of selling insurance like my dad or teaching like my mom, I wanted this." He sifted dirt through his fingers.

"You're like Thoreau, and this is your Walden Pond."

"'Let us spend one day as deliberately as Nature, and not be thrown off the track by every nutshell and mosquito's wing that falls on the rails,'" John quoted.

Phoebe applauded, her heart giving a little pitter pat at the gorgeous man quoting poetry to her. "My, my. A literary farmer."

He threw a bottle cap at her. "Not everyone needs to have a master's degree to be a nerd. I saw your face the first time you plugged in your typewriter."

"Oh really? And exactly what did my face tell you?"

"That you were having a nerdgasm over a typewriter."

"I feel the way about my thesis the way you feel about these fields," she pointed out. "Also, points for excellent word-play. You keep surprising me, John."

After the best pot roast he'd ever had—not that he'd be stupid enough to ever mention that fact to his mother—John buckled down to a different task at the kitchen table. His pen scratched quietly across the expanse of loose leaf paper in a satisfying production much different from how he spent his days.

Phoebe padded barefoot into the kitchen and opened the fridge to retrieve the bottle of wine she had stashed there the day before. He didn't have any wine glasses, but she made do with a water glass.

John noticed that she'd changed into shorts—very short shorts—and a t-shirt in royal blue with a V-neck. A deep one. She'd pulled all that long, sleek hair back into a ponytail high on top of her head. But it was the red framed glasses that grabbed at him. They were nerdy and sexy, rendering him desperate for a beer and a second shower. Both cold.

John shook his head at himself. His plan to get to know her better to become less attracted to her had essentially blown up in his face... or crotch. And now he liked her even more. A woman who was willing to put her own life on hold just to help out her family? That was Blue Moon through and through. He hadn't expected that from the ambitious Phoebe.

But that didn't mean he was going to change his mind about the rest of it.

Phoebe skipped over to her typewriter with her wine and the little notebook she carried with her. "Thanks for talking to me today," she said, sliding a leg over the chair and flopping down with a sigh. "I actually have some material I can work with."

He picked up the papers he'd stacked on the table and held them out over the typewriter. "About that. I think I have an idea."

Frowning, she pushed her glasses up her nose and began to read. Her gaze flew back to his, eyes sparkling.

"These are answers to some of the millions of questions I've thrown at you."

He scratched absently at the back of his head. "Yeah, I, uh, tend to communicate better in writing. I hope you don't mind."

She was out of her seat and hugging him before he could even put down his beer. He tensed against her, unprepared to have her lithe, soft body pressed against his. Dear God, she hadn't put a bra back on after her shower, and her breasts were in his face.

He gave her a little nudge backwards before she could find out what kind of effect she was having on him. He was only human.

"John, this is incredible," she said, smashing the papers against his chest, bouncing on her toes. "This is perfect!"

For the love of God, he needed her to stop bouncing. The shorts he'd changed into for the night were not hiding the hard-on that was currently throbbing for release.

Phoebe leaned down and placed a light kiss at the corner of his mouth. John didn't know what he was doing. One second he was trying to hold her off, convincing himself that they could remain platonic associates, and the next he was standing up so fast his chair tipped over backwards. The purely biological impulse took over and had him gathering her in to him.

Her eyes widened when he pulled her hips against him, and she felt him hard. Neither of them moved. John prayed that she would step away from him, make the decision for him. But God was not listening to the prayers of a terrified farmer. Still clutching the papers, Phoebe wound her arms around his neck. Her breasts, soft and warm, pressed against his chest and John's fingers flexed on her hips.

Phoebe felt better than he ever thought possible. She belonged here in his arms, his body decided, even as his mind argued. And if she moved again, John feared he wouldn't be able to be held responsible for his actions.

Oh, shit.

She rose on tip-toe. Her full lips parted slightly, her breath uneven. Those emerald eyes were bright and curious. He held his breath as she tilted her head to the side. Those perfect lips slowly, slowly began to close the distance between them.

His blood was on fire in his veins. He hadn't known he'd wanted this moment this badly until it was here. But now he knew. And he wouldn't forget again, wouldn't be able to bury the want, the thirst so easily.

Phoebe's lips grazed his, a delicate, hollowing touch. He prayed his knees wouldn't go weak and embarrass him.

He watched himself do it. Watched himself ignore the calculated, logical path he'd chosen and snaked a hand up to grip her ponytail. John tugged her head back so she was staring up at him, starry-eyed and trembling. A low growl, unlike anything he'd ever heard before, escaped his throat and sent Murdock scurrying down the hallway and up the stairs.

He was going to stake his claim, his blood pounding through his veins. The sharp tongues of anticipation, excitement, and need urged him on.

He was a millimeter from her mouth, those lush lips, those dark promises, when they both heard the pounding at the front door.

"Yoo-hoo?"

They broke apart like shattering glass. Phoebe sagged against the wall while John tried to will away the evidence of his desire and get his vision back from black.

"Holy hell," she breathed, her chest heaving with each gasping breath.

"I'm gonna need a minute here," he muttered.

"I can see that," she said, eyes wide.

The knock sounded again.

"I'll, um, go see who that is," she said, dazedly staring at his crotch and backing out of the room. She smacked into the doorframe and swore.

As soon as she was gone, John hustled across the room and shoved his head in the freezer. "What the fuck was I thinking?" he groaned to the ice cubes in the tray.

Phoebe Allen was a damn witch. There was no other explanation. She'd taken his understandable and logical reluctance to begin a relationship and seconds later had him mauling her in his own kitchen.

He was bewitched. And if he continued to think about her, the lust sparkling in her eyes, the breathy catch in her throat, he'd never be fit for company. Murdock was yapping at the front door now, and he heard a woman's voice. Maybe he'd just slip out the side door and gather his... thoughts.

ON AUTOPILOT, a scarlet-cheeked Phoebe yanked open the door.

"Hello, hello!" Elvira announced cheerfully as she bustled her way past Phoebe and into the house. "Hey, there little guy," she said, leaning down to scratch Murdock's head. The dog cowered for a second at this stranger's greeting before his little stub began to wag in a blur of ecstasy.

"I hope I'm not interrupting," Elvira said, straightening. "If I am, feel free to shove me right back out the door," she added in a conspiratorial whisper.

Phoebe finally found her voice. "Uh, no. Of course not. Not at all. You're not interrupting. We were just... talking... about the party." And now she sounded like a teenager lying to her parents.

"Perfect timing on my part then," Elvira congratulated herself and hefted the gigantic tote bag on her shoulder.

"Thought I'd come over and help you plan for the party Sunday."

She headed down the hall in the direction of the kitchen. "Got any wine?"

"Sure." Phoebe hustled along behind her and blew out a breath when she realized John and his impressive wood had escaped. She watched Elvira open and close cabinets in a quest for a glass. She found one and the wine and poured herself a healthy portion.

Phoebe mentally shook herself. *Get it together, dummy.*

She plastered a smile on her face. "Exactly how many people are coming Sunday?" Phoebe asked brightly.

Elvira made a humming noise. "About forty I think. Depends on if the Karlinskis are around or not.

"How many of them are there?" Phoebe asked.

"Twelve or thirteen," Elvira said, righting the chair that John had knocked over without comment. She sat and pulled a notebook out of her hemp tote.

"Twelve or *thirteen*?" Phoebe gasped, officially distracted from the revving engine her body had become at John's touch.

"Big family," Elvira shrugged. "The oldest two don't live at home anymore though. Cumulus joined the Peace Corps, and Raindrop works on Wall Street."

Phoebe decided it would just be easier not to comment on the "uniqueness" of the names. "Hmmm," she said instead.

All business, Elvira swiped the tip of her pencil over her tongue. "Now, I'm thinking burgers and hot dogs for the main course. That won't break the bank, and I know John has a grill. We'll spread the word and have everyone else bring a side dish or a dessert so the only other thing you two will need to worry about are beverages."

"Beverages," Phoebe repeated.

The side door to the kitchen swung open, sending

Murdock into another frenzy until he recognized John. Satisfied there was no threat, the dog plopped down on the floor and promptly began licking his own ass.

Phoebe's gaze tracked to John's shorts, and she was relieved and maybe the tiniest bit disappointed that all evidence of their near combustion was gone.

Well, not all evidence. There was nothing cool about those gray eyes now, she noted. There was a silent inferno burning between the two of them that Elvira seemed blissfully oblivious to. Their gazes held, and her breath caught. There was tension, thick and solid between them. The pull of a secret.

He didn't look angry, more annoyed. And Phoebe bet money that he was more annoyed with her than Elvira's poorly timed entrance. There'd be no going back, she decided. Not after how that almost-kiss felt. She would find a way into John Pierce's bed before the end of the summer whether he deemed it a good idea or not.

"There you are!" Elvira chirped. "Phoebe and I are working on the menu for Sunday. You're probably going to need to stock up on a few non-food related items," she warned him.

John dragged his eyes away from Phoebe and gave his attention to Elvira. "Like what?"

"Toilet paper. Don't pull an antisocial bachelor move and not have enough toilet paper for forty guests."

"Forty?" John sputtered. "What did you do? Invite the whole town? I only have one bathroom."

"We'll make do," Elvira said, waving away his concerns. "No one knows how to party like Blue Moon."

John stomped out of the kitchen muttering under his breath. "I hope it fucking rains."

13

The damn woman kept sending him smoldering looks, which John only picked up on because he couldn't stop looking at her. Even now as they mucked Melanie's stall, he couldn't stop himself from looking at her.

He'd come within a heartbeat of making a mistake and had been rescued by Elvira's fortuitous arrival. And with all his resolve and his internal pep talks, John was no longer confident that he wouldn't be pushed into that mistake eventually.

All Phoebe had to do was walk out of the bathroom in a towel and it would be over. Or forget a bra again. Or lean too close to him when she asked him to pass the salt.

"You could use a haircut," Phoebe mused, startling John back to the present.

She was staring at him over sweet Melanie's swayback. "Before the party, I mean."

John shoved a hand through his thick hair. He'd meant to get it cut. He sporadically made it into the Snip Shack in town but had forgotten to schedule an appointment—as usual. "I don't have time to get into town between now and then," he muttered.

"I can cut it for you," Phoebe volunteered.

"You cut hair?"

"As long as you don't want some fancy Flock of Seagulls cut or feathering. I can handle the basics."

This felt like a trap, John thought.

Sure enough before dinner, she had him shirtless on the front porch, a towel draped over his shoulders and gleaming scissors in her hand as he stared at her breasts which were in his direct line of sight.

"You sure you know what you're doing?" he demanded as she threaded her fingers through his hair, and he felt his blood begin to simmer. *Down boy. She was cutting his hair, not giving him a lap dance.*

He winced when he heard the first snip. "Don't be such a baby," she said, snipping another section. Deftly, she worked her way around the back, fingers stroking as she tilted his head this way and that. She smelled like sunshine and showers. When she stepped between his legs to trim the front and her breasts loomed inches in front of his face, John felt his mouth go dry. He felt like he was in danger of falling into a trance-like state.

"Are we going to talk about that thing that happened in the kitchen last night?" she asked.

He flinched at the glint of sunlight on the shears in her hand, and she laid a hand on his shoulder. "Relax."

"Do *you* want to talk about that thing that happened in the kitchen?" he asked, finally finding his voice.

Her bare thigh brushed the inside of his leg, and he held his breath. She already knew what kind of an effect she had on his body. She'd seen it with her own two eyes the day before. She had to be messing with him.

"For a non-kiss, it felt pretty intense to me," she said conversationally.

Intense? Intense was the feeling of metal scissors grazing his scalp while she stood between his damn legs. She had him so tied up in knots John didn't know if he should be turned on or scared for his life.

"It shouldn't have happened," he said, his tone brisk.

"Now there you go being ridiculous again." She sighed, and he felt her breath in his hair.

He grabbed her wrist, moving the scissors into neutral territory. "Phoebe, please don't take this the wrong way, but I'm not interested in pursuing a relationship with you."

She never reacted the way he thought she would. This time, instead of getting mad or hurt, she laughed. "Don't take *this* the wrong way, but from where I was standing in the kitchen, it looked like you were *very* interested."

John got to his feet and pushed Phoebe down on the stool. "I don't think it's a good idea for us to get involved. Better?"

"But bad ideas are so much fun," she pointed out.

He closed his eyes and counted to ten, praying for patience.

"Your eye is twitching again."

"I *know* my eye is twitching," he snapped. "Look," he continued in a slightly calmer voice. "Every decision I make has infinite ramifications. And I don't think I ever got that until I started farming. If I choose the wrong fertilizer or buy the wrong seeds or choose the wrong crop, it could be disastrous."

"I get that. But I thought we were talking about sex?" Her pretty green eyes sparkled with amusement.

"I'm getting around to that."

"Could you get there a little faster?" Phoebe asked. "I'm

97

getting distracted by the view." She looked at his bare chest and bit her lower lip.

"Stop it."

"Stop what?" she asked.

"Stop intentionally driving me insane. We both know I'm attracted to you. I don't need to be a walking, talking hard-on to prove that."

"If we're attracted to each other I don't see the harm in exploring—"

"You also didn't see the harm in moving in with a stranger you'd never met for the summer. You lucked out with me. I could have been some kind of homicidal maniac farmer looking to add another pretty corpse to my cornfield cemetery."

Phoebe blinked those jade green eyes at him. "I don't know what to say to that."

"Good because I'm not finished. I'm responsible for you while you're here, and being responsible for you doesn't mean stripping off your clothes and... and..." He tripped himself up with a blood-pumping vision of taking off her clothes until there was nothing left between them.

"Having sex?" she finished for him.

"You didn't come here for sex," he pointed out. "You came here to write your thesis. And I didn't agree to let you stay in hopes that we'd end up in bed."

"Technically you agreed to let a guy stay here," Phoebe reminded him.

"Look. We both made a commitment. You work here for the summer, and I put up with your interrogation. What would happen to that commitment if we did pursue a physical relationship, and it didn't work out?"

"We're adults, John—"

"Think about it. One false move, and I'm out the help I

need around here for the season, and you're back to square one with your school work. That's not fair to either one of us. Just like with the farm, every decision we make has consequences, and I'm not willing to pay them. And having someone come in and ask me a million questions about why I did this or why I won't do that puts me on the defensive."

She nodded. "Okay, I can get that. But what makes you so sure it would end badly?"

"We can barely get through a conversation without arguing."

"We don't argue," she argued. "We have spirited discussions, and I think there's another reason besides the whole honorable host deal. What is it?"

She was a canny little witch. John shoved a hand through his half-trimmed hair. "It's stupid."

"Well, now I have to know." She crossed her legs and propped her chin on her hand. "Spill it."

John leaned against the railing and screwed up his courage. "I bought this place to start my future. It's important to know what you want. I wanted land and crops and work that I look forward to. But more, I wanted a place to raise a family. That's my plan, and I don't want to detour from that. When I bring whoever the future Mrs. Pierce is here, I don't want her facing any shadows from the past. I bought this place for her."

"Well, hell," she breathed. "How am I supposed to make fun of that? That's the most romantic thing I've ever heard," Phoebe pouted.

"So, you'll give me some breathing room and maybe wear some looser, longer clothes?" John was anxious to extract a promise from her. If she wasn't coming on to him, he could battle his attraction easier.

Phoebe laughed. She rose and pushed John back down

onto the stool. "I'm not done yet." When she lifted the scissors, John wasn't sure if she was talking about his hair or her pursuit of him.

～

JOHN'S WISH for rain on Sunday was in vain. *The day was sunny and warm just to spite him*, Phoebe thought smugly. It was a beautiful damn day. A sentiment repeated over and over again by the good-natured farming families that descended on Pierce Acres like hungry hippies to a picnic.

The front yard looked as though Woodstock and a Duran Duran concert had gone to war. There were hand crocheted vests, decades-old denim, fanny packs, and mile-high hair cut in gravity-defying layers.

Murdock had barked at the first twelve cars to arrive before giving up and hiding in Melanie's stall in the barn. Phoebe had wiped her damp palms on her shorts and slapped on a welcoming smile. John was determined to pretend this party thing wasn't happening and that their almost-kiss hadn't happened. He had entered a hibernation from reality.

Thankfully, Elvira's prediction had proved correct. Throwing a party in Blue Moon required very little preparation. Parties tended to evolve naturally as long as there was enough food and beer to outlast the crowd.

The empty tables they'd set up on the lawn an hour earlier were now buckling under the weight of side dishes, salads, and desserts.

It seemed like a lot more than forty people had shown up, and none of them looked like they were in a hurry to get down to farm business.

John manned the grill like a captain through a hurricane,

grimly and with stalwart determination. No one would accuse him of being a social butterfly, Phoebe thought with a grin as she shoved Mrs. Murkle's dish of potato salad in between the other two potato salads on the picnic table. Since confessing that he had no intention of acting on his attraction, he seemed to have doubled down on his commitment to remain a hermit, avoiding her like a former one-night stand he ran into in church.

She would have thought John's commitment admirable if she hadn't been too busy plotting ways to destroy it. She'd carefully chosen her outfit with that exact purpose in mind. Phoebe's denim shorts showed plenty of leg, and the scoop neck of her impossible-to-miss red tank top highlighted all the right curves. She wore her hair long and loose and was regretting it in this heat until she'd caught John's slow, head-to-toe scan of her.

She'd lowered her Wayfarers, winked, and strutted away as he swore ripely under his breath.

Torturing the man was as satisfying as surprising him, Phoebe decided as he fumbled a plate of hot dogs.

She made herself useful playing hostess to the crowd and introducing herself to every stranger there.

Phoebe was rearranging the three, five, and seven bean salads in order of bean count when a woman in striped culottes and a black tank top approached. Her hair was dark and huge like a soap star's. A peace sign charm bracelet jingled on her wrist. She walked with the confidence of a person who knew absolutely everything about everyone.

"Phoebe, darling! How wonderful to finally meet you," she said, opening her arms.

"Okay. Hugging when we meet." Phoebe was wrapped in a death grip.

The woman pulled back. "I'm Mrs. Jillian Nordemann, first

lady of Blue Moon," she announced grandly. "Your cousin Gwendolyn and I were college roommates."

It made sense that Gwendolyn and Mrs. Nordemann had connected. They each wore their own badges of weird. Phoebe's weirdo second-cousin Gwendolyn played the tuba at great-uncle Art's funeral and collected cat ceramics. Mrs. Nordemann had turned scheming and meddling into a full-time profession.

"Mrs. Nordemann, it's so lovely to finally meet you." Phoebe greeted the woman who had successfully manipulated John into believing Phoebe was a he.

"Now, I want to hear *all* about your stay so far. Has John been welcoming?" Mrs. Nordemann hooked her arm through Phoebe's and began a slow turn around the yard. John spotted them and glared at Phoebe as she smiled sweetly in his direction.

"He's been absolutely lovely. I couldn't have asked for a better mentor this summer," Phoebe declared.

"I am so happy to hear that," Mrs. Nordemann said hiding her smugness behind a satisfied smile. "How has he been entertaining you all the way out here?" She gestured broadly at the fields and hills.

Phoebe kept her responses guarded and left out all mention of any brewing sexual attraction. She also took great pleasure in seeing every ounce of color drain out of John's face when he spotted them walking arm in arm. The burger he'd been about to slide onto Hazel's bun landed in the dirt. She winked at him and went back to her conversation.

Phoebe filled Mrs. Nordemann in on second-cousin Gwendolyn's latest news—she was now breeding miniature pigs in the backyard of her duplex in Scranton, much to the dismay of her neighbors—and Mrs. Nordemann fed her the gossip on every person they passed.

Farmer Carson? He owned twelve pairs of overalls so he only had to do laundry once a month.

Betty and Linus Fitzsimmons? Rumor had it they were growing a special "crop" in their basement.

Minnie Murkle? She took a part-time job at the Snip Shack answering phones and sweeping up hair and spreading gossip without her husband knowing. Mr. Murkle preferred wives that stayed home and had dinner on the table every night.

"How does the whole town except for her husband know?" Phoebe asked.

"Blue Moon is good at keeping secrets from one or two people at a time as long as it's for a good cause," Mrs. Nordemann winked. "Now, what are your plans after summer?"

"Thanks to John, I should be able to graduate this summer. I've already had an interview with the USDA before I came up here. They've got a few openings to fill in August, and I'm hoping I get one."

Mrs. Nordemann stopped in her tracks. "The USDA? Where would you be working?"

"Oh, it could be anywhere. Washington, D.C. to start most likely."

"But why not stay here, dear?"

Phoebe laughed until she realized Mrs. Nordemann was not pulling her leg. "Here? I went to school for six years for this degree. I need to use it or my parents will brutally murder me."

"Well, why don't you just marry a farmer? I'm sure a good husband would appreciate his wife's education," Mrs. Nordemann suggested brightly.

Phoebe tripped over her own feet nearly taking a header into a fence post. "Uh. Um. Married?" she squeaked.

"Marriage is wonderful, and just think what an asset you'd

be to your husband's farm! Look at John, for instance. Why you and your education could do him a world of good what with him living out here all by himself."

"You think I should *marry John?*" Phoebe wasn't feeling so well anymore. The potato salads that she'd sampled sat like bricks in her stomach.

Mrs. Nordemann giggled and then proceeded to flatten Phoebe like a steam roller. "Well, I certainly wouldn't want you to marry him if you didn't have feelings for him. You do, don't you? I mean, *of course* you do. I can tell by how you two look at each other. Married women can see such things. The smoldering glances, the whispered words of love." She sighed dramatically. "It *is* terribly romantic, isn't it? Young love. And he's so ready to settle down. It's just perfect timing."

If John had shot her smoldering looks, it was because he was pissed at her. And as far as whispered words of love, their communication was more akin to half-shouted insults. Yes, they had sparks. And those sparks would most likely ignite the sheets they lay on if he'd just give them a chance to get naked and enjoy each other. But *marriage?* That was a ridiculous idea. That was years off for Phoebe. First was graduation, then a job and paying her parents back. Then probably some travel. And then, *maybe*, if she found the right guy, she'd think about marriage. But it would be someone who supported her career, not tied her to a chunk of land.

Phoebe's panic level rose to new heights, and she felt like she was teetering at the top of a hill on a roller coaster. *Holy crap. What if they did have sex? Would John start sizing her up for marriage? Would she have to crush him like a bug if he gave her his heart?*

She felt sick. She'd been enjoying her little plan to seduce John so much that she hadn't really looked at the possible consequences. Sure, he'd expressed his concerns over consequences, but the idea that things would spontaneously combust between them leaving grudges and simmering anger? It was laughable. John Pierce was too good a man to allow something like that to happen.

She'd imagined a summer fling and a romantic goodbye, providing them both with sweet memories to treasure. But she hadn't considered what would happen if one of them wasn't ready to say goodbye.

Having to crush his dreams if things went *too* well between the sheets? To her, that was far more likely than an icy breakup leaving both partners without what they needed most this summer. And it was just like her to have not considered that in her pursuit of him.

Shit. Double shit.

Oblivious to Phoebe's internal turmoil, Mrs. Nordemann chattered on and on about fall weddings and the joys of life in Blue Moon.

"Oh, would you look at the time?" Phoebe held up her bare wrist to check the watch that wasn't there. "I'd better go see if the toilet paper roll needs changed."

14

"You got yourself a real fine roommate there, John," Alfie Cofax said between bites of his third hot dog. Alfie was scrawny as a scarecrow with tufts of red hair standing up on end and a face full of freckles. He looked to be about fourteen but had a few years on John. He also had a wife and three kids.

John hmmed noncommittally.

"Yep. I wouldn't mind chasing that around the corn fields," Alfie whooped in appreciation as Phoebe strolled by, hips swaying, hair swinging, this time with someone's distraught toddler in her arms.

"Isn't that your kid?" Michael Cardona asked, elbowing Alfie in the gut and nodding at Phoebe.

"Ah, crap. I forgot I was supposed to be watchin' him." Alfie chased after Phoebe leaving John and Michael alone at the grill.

"He's not wrong, you know," Michael said, admiring Phoebe's long legs.

"Don't start, Cardona," John growled a warning.

"I'm just stating a fact. She's a good-looking woman.

People are going to notice. Unless of course they're brain dead." Michael sent John a pointed look that he ignored. John slapped another row of burgers on the grill and pretended it was Michael's face.

"You know what I think?" John picked up his beer.

"What?"

"I think I need a new beer," he said, wiggling the empty can.

"Dude, seriously. Why aren't you moving on that?" Michael asked, exasperated. "It's like Hot Girl Heaven delivered an angel straight to you, and you're too dumb to make a move."

"I'm not too dumb to make a move. I'm not looking for a good time with no potential. End of summer comes, and she's out of here. Or worse, things blow up mid-summer, and I'm left without the help I need around here. Besides, I'm starting to think about permanent."

Michael looked at him as if he'd just announced he was going to grill up one or two of the smaller guests. "Permanent? Like marriage?" he scoffed.

John shrugged. "I don't know. Maybe. Not now, but when I have this place up and running at capacity in a few years, why the hell not?"

Michael slapped a hand on his shoulder. "John, I'm fearing for your mental health."

"Aren't you sick of chasing women, yet? Don't you wonder what it would be like to come home to the same face every day? Have kids, build a life? I'm too old for fucking around, and you should be too."

Michael snorted. "If I ever get too old for fucking, run me over with your shitty tractor."

"With pleasure. I could take care of it today," John offered.

"You know, since you're not interested in Phoebe, I think I'll ask her out."

"Why am I even friends with you?" John muttered, moving another group of hot dogs over to a plate and tossing a blackened one to Murdock who was cowering under the porch stairs.

"Who knows," Michael shrugged. "You'd probably get more girls if you didn't stand so close to me and all my prettiness."

"You're such a dick," John muttered. "And if you don't shut the fuck up about Phoebe—who is permanently off-limits as far as you're concerned—I'm going to tell you what I've been avoiding mentioning since senior year."

"Oh, really? And what's that? What life-changing advice do you have for me, Pierce?" Michael prodded.

"I think you were really into Hazel Garfunkle, and her shutting you down in high school crushed you. So, you've spent the last ten years trying to look like a big shot." He shoved the plate and his empty beer into Michael's hands. "And until you man up and tell her how you really feel— without coming across like an asshole—and what you really want, you're still going to be laying there at night thinking about her instead of whoever you talked into your bed that night. Now, go take these over to Phoebe without saying anything sexist or flirty to her and get me another beer."

"I like you better when you stick to one-word answers," Michael muttered.

"Yeah, well that makes two of us. This is what happens when I share a roof with a woman who talks a mile a minute about eighty-two different things."

"You're making me take these to Phoebe so you can avoid her, aren't you? Man, she must scare the shit out of you."

"Shut up and go away."

∼

PHOEBE'S PLATE of tabbouleh bean salad and tofu casserole slipped from her hands to the ground, landing facedown with a wet splat. Murdock scampered over, sniffed once, and decided he was better off waiting for another hot dog. She blinked, not trusting her eyes.

"Mom? Dad?"

"Surprise, sweetie!" Her mother's Charlie-scented embrace was overwhelmingly familiar. The sleeveless navy dress with the starched Peter Pan collar was one of her mother's favorites. And it too sent the sudden sting of homesickness through Phoebe.

"I can't believe you're here! What are you doing here? Oh, I've missed you guys. Dad! You're on your feet!"

Her father, dapper in an indigo golf shirt and checkered shorts, leaned heavily on his cane and beamed at her behind his thick sunglasses. Phoebe gave him a peck on the check. "Can't keep an old guy like me down. How's my little girl?" he asked with so much affection that Phoebe felt like holding on to him forever. He smelled like Old Spice.

"They aren't working you too hard, are they, my girl? Because you can always come home if you want to. I sure miss seeing your pretty smile at the dinner table. We'd be happy to keep you forever." Her father, the overprotective father figure, took his role so seriously that Phoebe and Rose had found themselves periodically grounded for their friends' offenses. A deterrent, Denny Allen had insisted. His little girls were going to stay his little girls forever.

"Oh, Dad. I missed you, too!"

"Now, don't let me hog you all to myself. We brought rein-forcements," he announced, waving with his free arm toward two others.

"Rose?" Her sister, hair freshly permed, was staring adoringly up at the man next to her. He was thin and lanky. His nose was too big for his face, and his hair was already going wispy, but his smile was wide and friendly.

"Missed you, sis," Rose said, tearing her gaze away from her beau so she could embrace her sister.

"Oh, I missed you so much," Phoebe sighed.

"Sorry, I didn't have time to give you a warning," Rose whispered in her ear. "We went out for breakfast today after church, and Dad got it in his head that we should drive up here and surprise his little girl."

Warning. Danger! Oh, shit. Phoebe was supposed to be living on a *family* farm with a family. Not under the roof of a sexy *single* farmer who made her feel like a volcano about to erupt.

"Oh, crap," Phoebe gasped.

"Think fast." Rose squeezed her arms before pulling back. "And this is Melvin, the man I was telling you about," she said in a louder voice.

The way her sister said Melvin's name was reverential as if Pink Floyd had wandered into the picnic looking to use the bathroom, and Phoebe snuck a peek to see what her father's reaction was to Rose's lovesick puppy routine. She caught him, pointing his fingers at his own eyes and then back at Melvin. "I'm watching you," he mouthed.

Melvin swallowed hard.

Phoebe greeted the terrified man and hoped all the right pleasantries were spilling out of her mouth while her brain worked on the problem at hand.

She needed a family willing to lie for her and she needed one fast.

"I hope we're not interrupting anything," her mother said, taking in the colorful crowd with a rather dazed look. Phoebe knew it well. It was the "introduction to Blue Moon" look when the mind tried to reconcile the past living in the present.

Clayton ambled past them in a brown fringed vest with two plates overflowing with hot dogs and potato salad. The circumference of his dark, full hair parted the crowd. He winked at her mother. "Better get some grub while it's hot," he said in his smooth-as-bourbon baritone.

"The Pierces are having a picnic," Phoebe lied brightly, the lie tightening her throat like an invisible noose.

"What kind of place is this?" her dad asked, staring blankly at Rainbow and Gordon who were making out against the door of a VW Bug painted like a smiley face.

"Mom, Dad, you guys stay right here. Grab a plate and stay *right here*. I'm going to go find the Pierces."

She dashed off before anyone could stop her.

Phoebe found John flipping burgers on the grill, surrounded by a loose circle of friends. She paused just long enough to take in the view, a vision of masculine sex appeal in faded denim and comfortable plaid. This might be her last look at him if her parents found out about her scheming, and she was determined to make it count. She may be an adult, but her father wouldn't hesitate to throw her in the trunk of the family car and drive her all the way home, lecturing her on common decency. Master's degree be damned.

"John, I need you."

The look he leveled on her said far more than words. She knew exactly what he thought she wanted. And given the way her pulse leapt, he wasn't off base. But there were more urgent conversations to have. She slapped him in the shoulder and then turned to make sure her family hadn't witnessed the exchanged. "Now is not the time for that!" she hissed.

He leaned in, keeping his voice low. "Word of warning,

don't start conversations with 'John, I need you,' unless that's exactly what you mean."

She flushed scarlet and began again, this time through gritted teeth. "I need you to pretend to be married."

"*Married?*"

She didn't even give him a chance to hand over the tongs. Phoebe was already dragging him back into the crowd. She had a farmer. Now, she needed a wife. Someone close to John's age... *Perfect.*

Elvira was restocking the coolers with ice and drinks along the side of the house. Phoebe hauled John with her.

"I wish to hell Coke would have just left well enough alone," Elvira muttered, dumping a six-pack of New Coke into the cooler.

"El, I've got a huge favor to ask. I need you to be married to John and living here."

Elvira looked up from the beverages. "For how long?"

"That's your first question?" John asked. "How about *why?*"

But Phoebe was busy building a family. "Hang on. You guys need a kid or two..."

"Phoebe!" John didn't sound amused.

"Stay!" she ordered and took off again.

Then she spotted the boy. He was skinny and squinty and wore glasses bigger than his own face. His parents were heaping brownies and mac and cheese on his plate. "There you go, Billy," his mother said cheerfully as she ladled another scoop on to the already dangerous peak of pasta.

"Excuse me," Phoebe cut in. "Do you mind if I borrow your son for a minute?"

"You're not going to do any weird mind experiments on him are you?" His father, rocking a sleeveless turtleneck and bellbottoms, laid a protective hand on Billy's shoulder.

"No, of course not. But I am going to ask him to pretend to be someone else's kid for a little while." She winced, waiting for the no that any parent in their right mind would give.

"Oh, that's fine. He does that on his own sometimes," the mother announced. She had the kind of friendly, vacant expression that reminded Phoebe of a happy-go-lucky coma patient. "Billy, you go with this nice lady and pretend someone else is your mom, okay?"

Phoebe felt a twinge of guilt and hoped she wasn't scarring the poor kid for life.

"Billy, there's chocolate cake in this for you if you pretend John's your dad and Elvira's your mom."

The kid nodded solemnly and then let out an ear-piercing scream.

"Oh, my God! Are you okay? Did you get stung by a bee?"

He shook his head. "Sometimes the screams just hafta come out," he announced.

Well, it was too late to find a non-screamer now, Phoebe thought.

"Do you still want cake?"

"Sure."

"Okay. One wife, one kid. I think we need another kid. What do you think?"

She flinched reflexively when Billy opened his mouth and then relaxed when words, not screams, came out.

"How about that one?" He pointed in the direction of the oak tree.

"Where did you get a baby?" John demanded when she returned, two children in tow.

"The kid was sitting unattended in a playpen under a tree. Maybe this will teach the parents to keep a closer eye on their children," Phoebe snapped. She shoved the baby into John's arms.

"Have you lost your damn mind?" John asked, bouncing the baby when she... or he started to fuss.

"Maybe. I'm not sure. My parents just showed up on your lawn. They think I'm staying on a family farm with a family, not living in sin with a sexy bachelor."

"Sexy bachelor?" John asked.

"Don't you actually have to be 'doing it' for it to be considered living in sin?" Elvira asked.

Phoebe covered the baby's ears. "Not in front of... John Jr."

"I'm pretty sure that's Millie Karlinski," Elvira corrected her.

"Fine. Look, please do this for me. My parents are old-fashioned. They would not approve of me staying here and I need this. They need this," she pleaded.

"You owe me big time, you little liar," John said, pointing his finger in her direction. The baby grabbed it and shoved it in her mouth.

"Watch out there. Some of those Karlinski kids are biters," Elvira warned him.

"Huddle up, everyone. You are John and Elvira Pierce, and these are your kids Billy and Millie Pierce. One big happy family."

Elvira ruffled Billy's hair. "How's it going, son?"

Billy let out a bellow and then grinned. "Fine, Mommy!"

"Maybe we should get this one something to eat so he can't say anything," Elvira suggested.

Michael Cardona sauntered up, enjoying a piece of chocolate cake. "Hey Blue Jeans," he said with a long, slow wink at Phoebe.

"Perfect!" She yanked the plate out of his grip and handed it over to Billy. "Stuff your face, don't scream. Got it?"

Billy shoveled a forkful into his mouth and nodded in delight.

"Hey, that's my cake," Michael argued.

"I'll get you another piece, but for now, I need you to go someplace else." She shoved him toward the barn.

"Hazel's over by the horseshoe pits," John said with a cocky grin.

Phoebe grabbed him by the wrist and wrangled the newly formed family in the direction of her parents.

"Mom, Dad, I'd like you to meet the Pierces," she said, breathlessly. John squeezed her hand hard, and it reminded her that she was still holding it. She dropped it like it was on fire. "This is John, his wife Elvira, and their son Billy and daughter Millie." *Shit. She should have renamed the baby.*

15

*B*esides her father insinuating that perhaps the Pierces were working his little girl too hard and the blood-chilling fear that John would sell her out just to get rid of her, the introductions went reasonably well.

Word must have spread like wildfire because she suddenly had an entire town weaving a backstory for her.

Farmer Carson loudly told her father he had officiated John and Elvira's wedding back in 1975, which would have made Elvira right around thirteen. However, no one except for Phoebe seemed to be doing the math.

Rainbow, who had finally dislodged Gordon's tongue from her throat called out a cheery "Hi Mr. and Mrs. Pierce," on her way to the food tables.

But Phoebe was convinced that the jig was up when she saw Sheriff Garfunkle approach with Michael Cardona. *She was about to be arrested for lying her ass off. She just knew it.*

"Phoebe, thanks so much for watching all the kids so we could go to dinner with John and Elvira the other night." Hazel Garfunkle smiled winningly as she dragged Michael into their circle. "We really appreciated having a date night."

Michael "Mr. Smooth" Cardona turned an interesting shade of baby pink and nodded until Phoebe thought his head might snap off his neck.

Phoebe managed to choke out a "Ha. No problem. Ha. Ha." She couldn't seem to stop laughing until Rose kicked her.

"Michael and Hazel have four kids," Elvira lied, stepping into her role as the fictitious Mrs. Pierce and making the introductions to Phoebe's family.

Michael's head bobbed again, and he made a choking noise.

John clapped him on the back and grinned. "You okay there, Cardona?"

"Just great."

Phoebe was just starting to enjoy herself when she spotted striped culottes heading their way. *Ah, crap.*

"You must be Denny and Diane," Mrs. Nordemann said, shoving her way into the circle. "It's so lovely to see you again. This is just like a family reunion!"

Phoebe again made the introductions and held her breath until her vision started to go black. There was no way to predict on which side Mrs. Nordemann's loyalties lay. On one hand, she was family. On the other, she'd made it clear that marrying Phoebe off to John was her goal this summer.

Phoebe felt a nudge in her back and turned.

"Kid's almost done with his cake," John hissed in her ear.

Like clockwork, Billy opened his chocolate smeared mouth and let out a blood-curdling shriek. Phoebe clapped a hand over his mouth as her parents looked on in horror. "Ha. Ha. I think that means it's nap time. Ha." This time Rose elbowed her in the side. "How about I put the kids down for their nap, and you can show my family around, Elvira?"

Her friend smiled nicely for their audience. "I'd love to,"

she said through gritted teeth. She leaned in. "Are you fricking crazy?"

"Please, please, please. Mrs. Nordemann might be about to sell me out, and if she doesn't, someone is going to come looking for this baby, accuse me of kidnapping, and then I'll be dragged back home left to spend the rest of my life wondering how everything would be different if I'd gotten my degree and moved out of my parents' house."

"I don't know anything about farming," Elvira hissed back.

"Perfect, neither does my dad. Just sell it, and I'll be indebted to you for life."

Elvira turned back to Phoebe's family. "I'd be happy to show you around. Have a good nap, kids." She patted Billy awkwardly on the head, and John shoved the baby into Phoebe's arms.

"If you'll excuse me, I left the grill unattended," he announced.

Coward, Phoebe thought as she watched him high-tail it away from the mess.

Elvira led everyone off in the direction of the barn, and Phoebe cringed when she heard her friend's comments about the barn. "Now this here's the butter churning area," Elvira said, gesturing toward the door to the barn. "It's a sterile room so I can't show you inside."

"If I get through this, I promise to hardly ever lie anymore," Phoebe promised the heavens as she deposited Millie back in her playpen and directed Billy back to his parents.

"Oh, there you are son. I wasn't sure if we brought you," his father said.

"Don't mind him. He's an over-indulger," Ernest Washington whispered to her with a wink as he breezed past. "Also, don't eat brownies made by a Fitzsimmons."

"Thanks for the tip."

Phoebe caught up with the tour just as everyone was coming out of the house. "And there you have it. Pierce Acres," Elvira was saying.

"You have a lovely home," Diane said. Her mother, still smiling, grabbed Phoebe's arm and dragged her off the porch. "You're living here alone with John?" she hissed.

"Oh, my God, Mom! How did you know?"

"There are no pictures in the house, no toys, no crib, and Elvira thought the linen closet upstairs was the bathroom before she opened the door."

"Does Dad know?"

"Sweetie, you know your father doesn't notice anything that isn't a direct male threat to his daughters."

"Are you going to tell him?" Phoebe asked in a bare whisper.

"Did I tell him about the time you skipped school to go to the Bangles concert?"

"No."

"How about the time I caught you and Rudy Walther making out in his dad's Camaro in our driveway?"

Phoebe cringed. "No, and I'm officially sorry for every terrible teenage thing I ever put you through."

"Then I'm not going to tell him about this either."

Phoebe wrapped her mom in a hug. "I love you, Mom."

"I love you, too, sweetheart. So, are you sleeping with John?"

"What? Mom! No!"

"Well, why not?" Diane asked, sneaking a look at John who was laughing over beer with Phoebe's father. "He's way better looking than Rudy Walther."

JOHN WAS RELIEVED when the last guests left at eight, the benefit of hosting an event on a Sunday in a farming town. If they'd done this on a Saturday, people would have stayed until dawn.

He and Phoebe worked silently through the cleanup, and he could feel her waiting for him to bring up her parents' surprise visit. She'd lied right to his face the day he met her, which, to his thinking, evened the score for his less than receptive welcome of her.

All her big talk about honesty and communication... He was enjoying finally being able to hold something over her head, and it was driving her nuts, judging by the confounded looks she kept sneaking his way.

He went up to shower, giving her a few more minutes to stew over her own deceit. And when he came back downstairs, she was at her typewriter, fingers flying over the keys. He slid his notebook paper out of the drawer, grabbed a ballpoint pen from the cup on the counter, and settled in across the table from her.

She raised her gaze, and he saw worried eyes behind the sexy red frames of her glasses.

Ignoring her, he set to writing. The tension pumping off of her was palpable, and he enjoyed it so much he thought about not saying a word until morning.

But she broke first. "Are you doing homework?" she asked, shoving her glasses up her nose.

He didn't bother looking up. "Something like that."

"We're not back to those answers again, are we?" Phoebe groaned.

John put his pen down and studied her. "It's something I do sometimes to unwind."

"What is?" she pressed.

"I write."

Now he had her full attention. He could feel her guilt over the lie move to the back of her mind, crowded out by curiosity. "Write what?" She leaned forward in her chair trying to see his paper over her mammoth machine.

"Just stuff," he shrugged. "Like what happens during the day."

"Like a journal?"

"This feels like badgering."

She held up her hands in peace. "Sorry. Just forget I'm here. Go back to what you were doing."

He picked up his pen and sighed. "I can feel you staring at me."

"What are you writing about?" she asked in a stage whisper.

"You sure you're not from around here? You have the nosiness nailed."

"Come on! Tell me."

"I'm writing about what a big fat liar my grad student is."

"Damn it! I *knew* you were going to throw it in my face," she screeched.

"Are you even in grad school, or was that another lie? Is your first name really Allen?"

"You would have sent me home if I told you the truth!"

"You're damn right I would. And I can't wait for you to have a kid that uses that excuse on you so you can hear how ridiculous it is."

"You know I needed this."

"Enough to lie to my face and then beg for my help when your big fat lie blew up in your face."

She put her head down on the table. "Things were so much easier when you were the one about everything."

"You know what's funny?" he asked, savoring the upper

hand for once. You're all 'female empowerment' until daddy shows up, and then you revert to a twelve-year-old."

"Force of habit. The man grounded *me* for two weeks when I was sixteen because my best friend got caught sneaking a boy into *her* basement to play seven minutes in heaven. I'm surprised he hasn't tried to chase off Melvin yet."

"You're an adult," he reminded her. "Don't you think it's childish and manipulative to still be lying to get your way?" It was like poking a hysterical bear.

"You do *not* understand what it's like to grow up with disappointing your parents being the worst punishment available."

Yeah, he did. But that's what good parents did.

"You lied to your parents, you lied to me, and then you forced me to cover for you." He shook his head. "I'm disappointed in you, Phoebe."

She groaned, looking to the ceiling as if wishing for divine intervention. When none came, she closed her eyes and took a deep breath.

"Fine," she said through gritted teeth. "I'm sorry for lying to you and making you pretend to be married to Elvira and stealing children. Happy?"

He grinned. "Yeah. I'm pretty happy."

"You're the worst person to apologize to," she grumbled.

"I'm sure it's just the first of many times," John said cheerfully. "You'll get better at it."

16

Mrs. Nordemann had gotten to her. Scared the hell out of her to the point that she was dreaming about the woman reciting the virtues of marriage. It had taken the fun out of her game, and Phoebe had put the brakes on her full court press of John, retreating into a sulky silence.

She'd been certain that she and John could survive a roll in the hay with their hearts intact, but if there was even the slightest chance that he could start eyeing her up as the future Mrs. John Pierce making her hurt the man who had opened his home to her and done his best to help her with her thesis? Well, then it was better to stay fully clothed and far, far away from him.

Unfortunately, her sudden reversal appeared to have piqued John's curiosity.

He was asking her half a dozen times a day if she was okay, and she'd caught him sneaking up on her to check on her. She assured him brightly that everything was just fine and he had nothing to worry about and then promptly went back to pretending he didn't exist.

Ironically, she'd made it to John's 4th of July deadline without a whisper of trouble. He apparently hadn't decided to send her home. He seemed to have finally accepted her ability to do pretty much anything on the farm that he asked.

With Murdock tagging along, they worked through the humidity of the morning and into the afternoon, checking crops, painting the north side of the barn, and now setting posts for a new fence line. Melanie would soon have a second pasture all to herself unless John fell for another homeless farm friend.

Phoebe took a slug of water and watched John swing the sledge hammer effortlessly down onto the last post, settling it into the gravel-filled hole. He was shirtless and slicked with sweat and not making her new resolution not to try to tempt him into bed any easier. She turned her back on him to stare out over the green that rolled out in all directions. She'd gotten to know part of his land these past few weeks.

She knew there was a creek carving through John's property just over the ridge, a pretty little bluff that provided a panoramic view of valley and fields. She'd captured that old stone barn from every angle in Polaroids. She shaded her eyes with her hand, studying the short stalks in their tidy corn field rows.

"Knee high by the 4th of July," she murmured to herself, remembering with a smile her grandfather quoting the adage every year.

"What's that?" John asked, swiping the jug of water from her and helping himself.

"Nothing."

John sat down on the open tailgate of his truck and sighed, squinting up at the sun. He looked so impossibly male sitting there, coated in sweat from a good day's work. "Guess we'd better get back to the house. Gotta get cleaned up for the festivities."

"Festivities?"

"Fourth of July. Picnic and fireworks in the park."

"We're going? Together?" she asked.

"You don't want to miss Blue Moon on the Fourth," he promised.

PHOEBE COULD FEEL the buzz of excitement in town as they made their way toward the park. John had insisted on driving. He claimed her driving was like watching a horror movie. She'd argued with him, but it hadn't been the first time she'd heard the criticism. Her sister refused to go anywhere with Phoebe if she was driving. But it was just one more reason to stay quiet in his presence. She wasn't about to engage in another argument with him. That's when her blood got stirred up.

John stopped three blocks back from the center of town and snagged a parking space. They got out, and he pulled an old quilt from behind his seat.

She looked at the blanket under the arm of a gorgeous man and then up at the darkening sky. The setup had romance written all over it. Was she supposed to snuggle up next to him on a blanket, watching the sky explode and not make out with him? "You know what, maybe I'll just go." She pointed back in the direction they'd come.

"Jesus, woman. What is your malfunction?"

Phoebe gaped at him.

"First, I can't get you to shut up, then I can't get you to stop flirting with me. Now, you act like I fell in Carson's manure pit and can't wait to get away from me."

This was not the John Pierce she'd met just a few weeks ago, the one who could barely string two words together.

"There's no malfunction. I just don't think it's a good idea to spend so much time together."

"See? That! That right there." He pointed his finger in her face. "What's that? When did that happen?"

"I thought you'd be happy about it," she said, matching his tone.

"I would be if I knew why you were suddenly clamming up around me. It makes me nervous, like you're plotting something."

"I'm not plotting *anything*. I'm just staying out of your way and not trying to get in your pants anymore!"

"Why the hell not? What changed?"

"Does it matter? I thought you wanted me to stay out of your pants!"

They were drawing a small, snickering crowd on the sidewalk, and John grabbed her hand and started dragging her toward the park. "You know what? You're right. I don't care. But you're not missing these fireworks even if you are exasperating and annoying."

He kept his grip on her hand, and she was glad for it when they got to the park. It appeared that the whole town had turned out. They wove their way in and out of blankets and people, dodging Frisbees and fast-footed toddlers.

John towed her over to a copse of trees next to the gazebo where a '60s cover band was warming up the crowd with the Beach Boys' "Good Vibrations." Michael, Elvira, and Bobby were sharing a pink blanket and a huge pizza.

"About time," Bobby complained. "I had to slap this one's hands away from your slices." She shot an accusatory look in Michael's direction.

"John gets crabby when I touch his stuff," Michael said with a long, slow wink in Phoebe's direction.

Elvira elbowed him in the gut. "Behave."

"Listen to my wife. She's very wise," John quipped.

"We're newlyweds." Elvira batted her eyes. "He thinks everything I do is adorable and perfect."

Everyone but Phoebe laughed. The joke was at her expense, of course. She'd begged John and Elvira to cover for her, pushing them into a fake marriage. But the idea of them actually being together wasn't funny to her. In fact, it made her feel a little sick to her stomach.

She pressed a hand to her stomach trying to will the feeling away. This damn man and his damn town had her so confused she didn't know which way was up.

"You okay there, Phoebe?" Bobby asked, handing her a slice of pizza on a paper plate.

"She's not feeling herself today," John said, cracking open a beer. Phoebe picked up on the undercurrent of annoyance in his tone.

"This will make you feel better," Elvira promised, handing Phoebe a plastic cup. "Spiked lemonade. The best of childhood and adulthood in one cup."

Phoebe sat and ate and drank. The grass in front of the gazebo had been cleared for dancing. Most of the dancers, she noted, were barefoot, and there was no age limit. Multiple generations hot footed it around with their sweethearts.

She did her best to smile even though she felt a headache brewing. It was because of this stupid roller coaster of attraction and a thousand solid reasons not to act on it. The marital jokes continued as did her bad mood.

No one likes a holiday downer, she reminded herself. She needed to get a hold of herself and enjoy the festivities of her only Fourth of July in Blue Moon.

"Since these two are old and married," Michael said, nodding toward John and Elvira. "What do you say you take a turn on the dance floor with me?"

Phoebe saw John's expression turn mutinous. "I'd love to." Her smile wasn't forced this time.

Michael gallantly pulled her to her feet, and they picked their way over and around picnickers to get to the band. "I can feel him staring daggers at me," Michael said, grinning down at her unperturbed.

Phoebe shook her head. "I don't know if I'll ever understand male friendships."

Michael slid his hands around her waist, and she held her breath, waiting for even the slightest spark. A brush of John's hand, and she trembled like her knees had earthquakes. A slow dance with the equally handsome and even more charming Michael? Nada. Life just wasn't fair.

"It's how we show our love for each other. By being dicks."

Phoebe laughed and noticed when Michael's gaze wandered to the edge of the dance floor. She followed it to Hazel Garfunkle. Hazel was out of uniform tonight. She wore shorts and a tank top and her blonde hair loosely braided under a stars and stripes bandana. She was laughing at something Bruce Oakleigh was saying to her.

Phoebe gave Michael a pinch. "Why don't you ask her to dance?"

"Who?" he frowned.

"Duh. Hazel. The woman you're always sneaking peeks at."

"I don't sneak peeks," he argued.

"Okay. The woman you slobber after. Ask her to dance."

"She'd just say no."

"Give her a reason to say yes."

He looked thoughtful. "Like what?"

"Tell her your biggest regret in life is that she turned you down for prom and that she owes you a dance."

Michael snorted. "Like that would actually work." He glanced in Hazel's direction again. "It wouldn't, would it?"

"Women like honest, and they like to know they matter. You don't have to dress it up."

"Mind if I cut in?"

Michael twirled her around so she was facing a grumpy looking John.

"Dude, if you can't slap a smile on your face, someone's going to slip you a special brownie," Michael warned him.

"Go away, Cardona."

"I got something to do anyway," Michael said, his gaze already on his target.

"Good luck," Phoebe called after him.

John slid his hands around her waist, and Phoebe instantly felt the frisson of energy at his touch. Why did it have to be him that made her feel this way? Why couldn't it be someone else in another couple of years when and where she was ready?

"Why aren't you dancing with your fake wife?" Phoebe snipped, hoping for at least some emotional distance.

"Is that jealousy I hear?" John asked, looking more amused than annoyed. It only pissed her off even more.

"You and this whole damn town have me all twisted up!"

"Me? What did I do?" he demanded.

"Nothing. Absolutely nothing. You say you're attracted to me, which puts thoughts—nice steamy ones—in my head. Then you don't want to jeopardize our 'working relationship,' which just makes me want you more because I can't have you. And then Mrs. Nordemann swoops in like a damn vulture and tries to convince me to marry you since you're all ready to settle down! So now sex is definitely off the table. But that doesn't stop me from not liking it when you flirt with other women."

John dipped her with more abruptness than finesse. "You're an intriguing woman, Phoebe Allen."

She held on tight around his neck. "Damn it, John."

"You really think that if I had sex with you, I'd be so overcome with desire that I'd have to marry you?"

When he put it like that, it sounded stupid. Really stupid. But she wasn't imagining the chemistry. That moment in the kitchen, the haircut, hell, right now her skin was burning up everywhere he touched her.

John pulled her upright and into him, fitting her body against his as they moved to the beat.

"Don't look at me like that, John."

"Like what?"

"Like you think I'm insane. Mrs. Nordemann—"

"Jillian Nordemann is a manipulative, string-pulling, pot-stirring, pain in my ass."

"I'll drink to that," a cheerful drunken hippie stumbled past them, raising his flask to John.

"She thinks I should marry you and move here." She worried her lower lip with her teeth.

"Is that why you've been acting like a weirdo since the picnic?" John asked.

Phoebe shrugged, not wanting to cop to falling for what now sounded like an idiotic train of thought.

"You think you're that irresistible?" he asked, those gray eyes dark and searching.

"Excuse me! Some people think I'm a catch," she argued. "To put it in terms that you'd understand, some men would be thrilled to be 'an item' with me."

"Guess you'll have to take Cardona off that list," John said, nodding across the dance floor.

Momentarily forgetting her own angst, Phoebe softened. Michael was dancing with Hazel, and the look on his face was positively sinful. Hazel didn't look like she minded it a bit.

"It's about damn time," John muttered.

"If it's about damn time, why haven't you done anything to help him in that direction?" Phoebe wondered.

"I did. I just told him to get his head out of his ass."

"Just told him as in recently?" Phoebe asked.

"Yeah. A week or two ago."

"What the hell took you so long? I was here all of a week when I realized he's head over heels for her."

"I let nature take its course," John shot back. "Things work out best when you don't try to force them."

"Or they never happen at all," she argued. "Sometimes things need a little push in the right direction."

"That's not the way I operate," he told her.

Phoebe rolled her eyes. "Oh, believe me. I know."

"And what's that supposed to mean?" Now he was getting annoyed.

"You're a plodder."

"A plotter?"

"P-L-O-D. You're not a mover and shaker. You don't make quick decisions because you're too busy weighing out every possible outcome."

"There are consequences to every decision," John reminded her, irritated.

"Yeah, yeah. And sometimes, when you spend all your time worrying about the consequences, you miss out on some really great opportunities because you think everything to death!"

"*What* are you talking about?" he demanded.

"Ugh. Forget it. Just forget everything." Phoebe pulled herself out of his grasp and stalked away.

She didn't want to go back to the blanket with her mood black as the darkening night sky. She wanted to be alone and fume in peace. She slipped around the gazebo and away from the merriment, cursing the crazy town's crazy vibes that were making her crazy.

The man was infuriating. He had a smart, interesting, attractive, *willing* woman—one that he admitted to being attracted to—under his roof for the next month, and John Pierce, with his glacier-like moves and 1950s etiquette, couldn't get beyond his pro/con list. If he wasn't worried about falling head over ass for her, then maybe he just wasn't interested. And he could have saved her a ton of angst by admitting it, letting her suffer her embarrassment, and then moving on.

She felt better, letting her temper guide her to a tree line just beyond the gazebo. On the other side of the park, hundreds of Mooners were anxiously awaiting their co-dependent town's celebration of independence. And she should be enjoying it with them. It was a once in a lifetime chance to be right here, right now. And she was wasting it moping over a man who was never going to make his move.

"What is my problem?" she asked the night.

"You lack patience. You need to know what you want *and* be patient enough to get it."

John's hands were on her, turning her to him. She opened her mouth to argue, to apologize, to promise she'd give it a rest. But the words never came out. John's mouth was on hers, softly, sweetly, with a steady undercurrent of determination.

17

---

*E*xplosions of color and fire lit the sky in a spectacular show. But it was nothing compared to what Phoebe saw when John's mouth covered hers. Softly at first, sweetly, his lips moved over hers. His fingertips held her face, still giving his mouth free rein to explore. The heat, the tenderness overwhelmed her. She was dizzy with it as he unglued her piece by piece.

Finally, when she thought she could take no more, John deepened the kiss. His tongue swept inside her mouth to taste and tease. Phoebe felt her toes curl into her sandals as if they were trying to hold her upright. She clung to him, fingers cramping from the strength of her grip on his shoulders.

She felt the booms of the fireworks in her bones, and the rest of her body vibrated with the need that John had ignited within her. His hands were on the move, sliding down her back to the curve of her ass. He squeezed, lifted, hitching Phoebe up his body. She wrapped her legs around his waist and enjoyed the new angle of the kiss.

Her brain completely blanked. All that registered was pleasure and need, and there was so much of both.

He pulled away even as she tried to drag him back, hold him still. "We need to go home. Now." His voice was jagged like shards of glass.

"God, yes."

Half stumbling, they made the mad dash to John's truck in the shadows, pausing only twice to fuse their mouths together again, hands wandering, fingers gripping.

He opened her door, feasted on her mouth until she was frantic, and then slammed the door shut in her face before racing around to the driver's side.

He jumped in, starting the engine before his door was even shut. Phoebe was already sliding across the seat to him.

"Do *not* distract the driver," he ordered.

Phoebe ignored the direct order and shucked her t-shirt over her head.

"Oh, sweet Jesus," he muttered, shooting her breasts a desperate look as they careened toward home.

"I've never seen you drive so fast," Phoebe murmured, returning her mouth to the tensile curve of his bicep. She nipped. "Usually you're so slow and methodical."

"If you don't behave, we're going to end up in a ditch."

"I don't care where we are as long as you're inside me."

"Christ. When you talk like that, it drives me insane. There's no blood left in my brain."

Phoebe slid her hand down his chest, over taut abs to the waistband of his Levi's. "I wonder where it all went?" Playfully, she yanked the button on his fly open.

"I think I'm going to black out." He pressed the accelerator down to the floor as they left the town limits. The old truck reluctantly picked up speed.

She drew down the zipper on his jeans with her last ounce of patience.

"Phoebe." There was a warning in there somewhere tangled up with breathless yearning.

"Just drive, John." She plunged her hand into the loosened waist band and breathed hot against his shoulder when she found him hard.

They were flying now at least as fast as the truck could manage, which wasn't much higher than the speed limit. But she was done waiting, done over-thinking, done letting him plot and plan and weigh his options. She slipped her fingers under the band of his boxers and gripped flesh, hot steel flesh.

The way John gritted out her name made her shaky and weak.

She bit her lip to keep the desperate noises that were clawing their way up her throat quiet. Determined to drive him to the edge, Phoebe stroked down from the crown of his cock to the thick root.

John cut the wheel hard to the left on an oath. She felt the truck slide, heard the grate of gravel churning beneath them, and felt the dull thud of an impact. "Close enough."

They were in his driveway—technically next to it—the tailgate gently kissing the fence post it had fishtailed into.

John cut the engine and lifted his hips, shoving down his jeans.

"Yes," she hissed, yanking his boxers with the jeans. And when he sprang free, one of those moans clamored its way out of her throat.

He was on her then, hands cupping her breasts through the lace of her bra, mouth tasting what her lips offered.

"We need to slow down," he murmured, against her jaw.

"No time." Phoebe fought his shirt over his head and licked and bit a path over his chest.

He sucked in a breath through his teeth which turned into a groan when she wrapped her tight fist around his shaft and stroked, pumping him hard enough to coat his blunt crown with moisture.

"Damn it." He shoved the straps of her bra off her shoulders and unhooked the closure. She spilled free into his hands and then his mouth was on her. First one tender peak and then the other. His desperate pulls had Phoebe arching her back, offering him more. Overwhelmed, out of control. That's how he made her feel.

He stroked the flat of his tongue over her nipple, and Phoebe's head fell back on her shoulders. She wanted this, to be awash in nothing but pleasure, sharp and jagged, and John was taking her there as if he already knew every secret desire she had.

"Are you still thinking of the future Mrs. Pierce?" she gasped out the words.

"I can forget about her for a night," he murmured against her breast. "Besides, technically we're not in the house."

She grabbed his face in her hands. "You're not going to want to marry me after this, are you?"

"God no. You're not my type," John promised.

Her laugh was breathless. He tore himself away from her mouth and feasted on her neck, making her tremble as his rough jaw stroked over her flesh. Her nipples, damp now, strained for more.

"I can't catch my breath," she whispered.

"You can have mine," he promised.

She sucked in an unsteady breath. "Please tell me you have a condom."

His mouth froze on the upper curve of her breast, just over where her heart hammered. "Fuck."

She shook her head. "I'm just messing with you. I have one in my pocket."

His head came up, gray eyes dark. "You're evil. You've been carrying a condom around with you?"

"Lucky charm. Do you want to argue about my optimism, or do you want to put my condom to use?" Phoebe settled the question by unbuttoning the fly of her shorts.

Even in the dark, she could see those gray eyes go molten.

"Take them off," he ordered, voice harsh.

There was no "please," no determination to go slow. She'd won, and that dark victory had her heart pounding, blood scorching its way through her veins. She would belong to him tonight, and he to her.

He bit her lightly on the shoulder, and Phoebe's fingers tremored when she retrieved the condom from her pocket.

"Here." She thrust it at him and, with more enthusiasm than finesse, rid herself of her shorts and underwear.

John tore the wrapper open and fumbled once, refusing to take his eyes off her. Phoebe grabbed the condom, and as she rolled it down that thick column of flesh, John licked two fingers and guided them between her legs.

"Oh, my God."

"Just you wait," he said darkly, sliding them into the wet heat of her core.

The invasion had her thighs trembling as she fought to stay on her knees. He pulled out and slid home again, Phoebe riding his hand as he moved.

"I want to touch you," she whispered, reaching for his hard-on.

"Later. I won't last if I give you free rein."

She was already quivering around his fingers, dangerously close to the edge. "I need you, John."

And then he was lifting her to straddle him, and she was opening for him. He thrust into her in one, smooth motion and then clutched her to him. For a second, Phoebe just felt.

The brutal fullness. The quick rise of his chest as it played over the tips of her breasts. The charge in her blood that begged her to move, to take.

He held her there, reminding her exactly who had taken her to this edge. And when he finally moved, finally stroked in and out of her, she was coming hard and bright, gripping his shoulders with all her might so she wouldn't come apart in his arms.

"Yes," he grunted as she rode him violently until the tremors subsided to little shivers of pleasure.

She collapsed against him for a moment, collecting her breath. Surprised to find his heart pounding in time with her own.

"More," she whispered against his neck.

He gave her more, one hand between her legs stroking her where she needed it. John leaned forward and latched onto her breast. His thrusts were faster now, and she could feel the build coiling within him. He was going to come, and she was going to take him there, wrapped around him, shattering with him.

She slammed down against his thighs drawing a satisfying groan from him. His hand gripped her hip hard, callused palms against smooth curves.

"Come for me again, Phoebe. Take me with you." His demand was a joy to fulfill.

Phoebe met his furious thrusts beat for beat, rocking her hips into him until sweat dotted her skin. The cab of the truck, their own personal pleasure den, was humid like a rain forest. She smelled him, that scent of wind and sun and sweat and straw. Felt his muscles bunch under her hands as his entire body tensed.

She was taking him over the edge. She tightened around him, and he made a desperate noise. He gripped her hips with both hands and slammed her down on his cock holding her there. His muscles froze, and she felt him come. His shout was triumphant, and it dragged her over the cliff after him. With him fully sheathed in her, her orgasm bloomed, and then he began to move again, thrusting through each shattering wave they shared until there was nothing left to give, and she was like water in his arms.

~

THE SOUND of a horn brought them back from the orgasmic abyss. The mental fog of satisfaction was so thick, it took a full ten seconds for Phoebe to realize it was her ass resting against the steering wheel that was making the horn sound.

John lifted her off the wheel.

"Did that just happen?" Phoebe murmured against his neck where she'd buried her face. His rough fingers trailed up and down her back in delicious, feather-light strokes.

"Yeah, it happened."

"You don't sound pleased. Are you mad?"

She felt rather than heard his laugh. "I don't see how someone could be human and be mad after *that*."

"But this wasn't your plan," she pressed.

John's fingers found their way into her hair, combing their way through, still gentle.

"Maybe there's something to be said about a detour. You know me, I like to work with nature rather than against it."

"This was very natural," she said, a sexy smile spreading her swollen lips. "No regrets?"

"Just one."

Phoebe lifted her head to look into his eyes. He was relaxed, thoughtful, and still touching her in slow, sweet strokes. "What's your regret?"

"That I didn't listen to you sooner."

She laughed and pressed a kiss to his closed lips. "Repeat after me. Phoebe is always right."

He tickled her instead, and she got a funny feeling in her stomach when he flashed that crinkle-eyed grin. They were still joined, and the moment was so intimate it gave her pause. Mrs. Nordemann's words echoed in her head. *He's ready to settle down. Why don't you stay here?*

From where she sat, with him still inside her, the idea didn't sound quite as ludicrous. And that was what prompted her to lift off of John's lap and slip onto the seat next to him. She needed to break that connection, or she'd end up broken hearted at the end of the summer.

John would fall for a different kind of woman. One who thrived on long silences and the quiet isolation of farm life. She had different plans for herself, different needs. As long as she could keep a sliver of distance between them, they could part ways at the end of the summer. Each free to pursue the future they'd planned.

He ran a finger over the line between her eyebrows. "Deep thoughts?"

"Anyone who has the power to think after that is inhuman," she declared.

"I find your silence disconcerting," he teased. "I like it better when you're blurting out everything that goes through your mind."

She laughed and leaned in to hug him. "Bet you wouldn't have thought you'd feel that way when we first met."

He grinned at her, and she pressed her face to his shoulder to quell the quiver in her belly.

"I have a question," she confessed to his skin.

"What's that?"

She trailed her teeth up his neck and over the edge of his jaw. "Can we do it again?"

He held her by her forearms. "Hang on, insatiable. Let's talk a minute."

"What's there to talk about?" she asked innocently.

"Phoebe." He said her name with a world weariness. "That was a big decision we just made. Let's lay some ground rules."

"No sex in the house?" she offered, thinking of the future Mrs. Pierce.

John stared down at her breasts that she'd neglected to cover. "I think it will be easier if I just tear down the house and start over."

"Okay, good. Because I don't want to get hay in my crevices. What else?"

"What does this mean?"

She laughed and rubbed her nose against his cheek with affection. "Isn't that my line?"

"It appears I'm the only one concerned with the long-term effects of this."

He was dead wrong, but she wasn't about to get into all that and ruin the afterglow. "What do you want this to mean?" she asked, linking her hands behind his neck.

He shrugged. "I may be able to eventually wrap my head around temporary, but I can't do casual."

"So, monogamous then?" Phoebe clarified.

"Hard line."

"Agreed," she said cheerfully.

"You make it sound like we're deciding on appetizers."

"If *that* was an appetizer," she said, gaze sliding to his crotch, "I may not survive the entrée."

He pinched her. "Be serious for five seconds, please."

"John. I like you, you like me. We know this can't go anywhere beyond the summer. Let's just be okay with that and enjoy it. I want to look back on you as my most memorable summer. Everyone should have a summer love that they remember forever."

"That doesn't sound so bad," he admitted.

"You can name your next rescue cow after me."

18

*P*hoebe strolled through the town square, a fresh donut decked out in a rainbow of sprinkles from the bakery warm in her hand. Elvira hailed her from outside the record store.

"Pheebs!"

Phoebe waved and headed in her friend's direction.

"Did John give you the afternoon off?"

Phoebe grinned, finishing her bite of sugary perfection. "He's doing the books and claimed I was distracting him."

She'd sailed through the kitchen buck naked while he sweated over ledgers with a pencil and stack of receipts. The receipts and ledgers had been swept off the table and replaced with Phoebe's ass until John came to his senses.

"Just give me the afternoon," he had begged. "I swear I'll make it worth your while."

She had no doubt of that. So, it was off to Blue Moon to while away the afternoon. Her thesis was finally in completed draft form and sitting on John's nightstand. He'd promised to read it this week, but Phoebe was in no hurry. Now that it had taken shape, it was mostly just polishing to do. And now that she'd found her way into John's bed, she wasn't in any hurry to find her way out.

Elvira fell into step beside her. "Okay, I've waited the appropriate amount of time to ask what happened last night. You two disappeared and missed the fireworks." Her dark eyes sparkled with the anticipation of steaming hot gossip.

"Oh, believe me, we saw fireworks," Phoebe said, offering Elvira half her donut.

Elvira grabbed it. "I knew it! How was it?"

Phoebe rolled her eyes back into her head as she had with the first bite of donut and Elvira squealed.

"Oh, my God. Okay, wait. Don't tell me yet. This deserves some coffee. Let's hit the café."

"What café?" Phoebe asked, scanning the street in both directions. She'd been in the town square a dozen times in the past month and never noticed a coffee shop.

Elvira pointed at the Airstream trailer, the sunlight glaring off its metal body, taking up three parking spaces in front of the movie theater. It had a green and white awning stretched out over two tiny café tables.

"No. Way. That's a café?"

"Not a legal one," Elvira said, adjusting her sunglasses. "Which is great because not being bound by the law means Dixie, the proprietor, stocks up on liquor store minis. How do you feel about an Irish coffee?"

"I feel like my soul demands one. And possibly another donut."

"You grab the baked goods, and I'll get us a table before someone beats us to it."

Five minutes later, Phoebe was perched on a rickety folding chair enjoying instant coffee heavily laced with whiskey and Irish cream.

Elvira took a bite of Danish and sighed. "Okay, now, spill."

Phoebe filled her friend in with a high-level review of last night's escapades.

"He drove into his own fence?" Elvira cackled, slapping the table. "Can I ask him about the damage next time I'm out? Can I please?"

Phoebe bit her lip. "Maybe I shouldn't have said anything. We haven't exactly decided to broadcast it."

Elvira pressed her lips together and made a locking motion. "My lips are sealed."

"You're from Blue Moon. Your lips are never sealed."

"Not true! We keep all kinds of secrets around here."

"Example?" Phoebe challenged her, taking a sip of her coffee. "And don't use Minnie Murkle and the Snip Shack."

"Well if you're going to put restrictions on it, I'm going to need some time. Let me get back to you on that one. In the meantime, tell me what this all means. Are you staying? Are you guys together? What about your master's and a job?"

Phoebe reached for an apple fritter. "Well, I guess the only thing that's changed is we're sleeping in the same bed now. I'm still getting my degree, and I'm still looking for a job."

Elvira settled her elbows on the table and leaned in. "Why not work here?"

Phoebe shook her head. "I need cash. A lot of it."

"Bookie problems? Is someone going to break your kneecaps?"

"I wish it were that simple. My parents need the money. And if Nordemann knows this, how do you not know it?"

"She never breathed a word! I'm going to remind that woman of her duties as Town Busy Body. There's a lot of competition for that title."

Phoebe shook her head and filled Elvira in on her parents' predicament. "If I don't get a job and start contributing now, they'll lose the house," Phoebe told her.

"Oh, sweetie. I'm sorry to hear that." Elvira reached out and squeezed her hand. "It's hard to see parents go through a tough time."

"They've dedicated their lives to making sure my sister and I have everything we needed. It's our turn to give back, and as soon as I get a job, a good one, I can start chipping away at the twenty grand in medical bills."

"Ouch. Your parents are lucky to have you as a daughter." Elvira raised her coffee cup. "To family."

Phoebe clicked mugs with her. "To family," she echoed. "What about your family? Do they live here?"

Elvira shook her head. "My mom moved to Boca after she and dad got divorced. He lives in Wisconsin with his third wife. I have an older brother in the city."

"Why did you stay here?"

Elvira's smile was warm. "I can't imagine living anyplace else. I may not have blood here, but I do have family."

"Do you want to get married? Have a family of your own?" Phoebe pressed.

"God no! Not after the shit show my parents put on," she grinned wickedly. "I like being exactly who I am without worrying about fitting someone else into my life."

"That's very Blue Moon of you," Phoebe winked.

"What if staying here was an option?" Elvira mused.

"You mean what if $20,000 fell into my lap, and I could go wherever I wanted?"

"Dream big," Elvira advised.

Phoebe lifted her shoulder. "I don't know. I've been on this path so long. I was going to go into research, you know, help identify new technologies, new biochemistry applications."

"Stop it with your farm geek speak," Elvira laughed, pretending to fan herself.

Phoebe grinned and bit her lip. "I don't know. There's

something so hands-off about that side of things. You know? I've spent the last few weeks hands-on. Up to my elbows in dirt and produce and weed spray and... I love it."

"Ladies," the smooth baritone of a world class flirt interrupted their conversation. Michael Cardona grabbed a chair from the other table and pulled it up to their table, slinging a leg over the seat. He helped himself to a piece of Phoebe's fritter.

"Help yourself," Elvira snorted.

"Is that Cardona out there?" Dixie, her cloud of white hair framing an unlined face like a halo, yelled from the door of the Airstream.

"It is, Ms. Dixie," Michael said fixing his most flirtatious smile in place.

She rolled her eyes. "Save it for someone ten years younger. I suppose you'll be wanting a coffee?"

"Yes, ma'am," he called. Dixie disappeared back into the trailer.

"What brings you out today?" Phoebe asked Michael.

"Sheer boredom. Four days without a call. No fires, no accidents, not even a damn ferret stuck in a tree."

"That's because you made Alfie promise to keep his pets on a leash after the last time," Elvira pointed out.

"I didn't realize that would lead to a life of boredom," Michael sighed heavily. Dixie returned, shoving a mug of steaming black coffee into his hands.

"Thanks, Ms. Dixie."

"Save it, Romeo." She bustled back into her cocoon, and Phoebe could hear a newspaper crinkle.

"How did your dance with Hazel go last night?" Phoebe demanded.

The tips of his ears turned pink. "Are you blushing?" Elvira gasped, pushing her sunglasses down her nose. "Well, as I live and breathe, Michael Cardona is speechless and turning pink!"

"I am not!" Michael rubbed the tip of one ear. "It's the sun. Shut up."

"You liiiiiike her," Phoebe teased.

No one missed the upturn of his mouth. "Shit. Okay. Yeah. I like her, and the dance was... nice."

"Which one?" Elvira grinned wickedly, twirling a curl around her finger.

"You danced with her more than once?" Phoebe gasped.

Elvira held up three fingers.

"No, way!"

"How did you miss that, nosy?" Michael shot back.

"Oh, Phoebe and John had their own personal fireworks show to watch," Elvira smirked.

Michael's grin was blinding. "No, shit? You and John." He held up his palm, and Phoebe pretended to be the slightest bit reluctant about slapping it.

When had she done this last? she wondered. Had coffee with friends, caught up on lives? There wasn't a lot of camaraderie in her major, at least not for a woman. She'd had casual acquaintances in school, sure. Girls she met for drinks or study partners. But when had she had real friends who talked about real things? And who would have thought she'd find those relationships in the little town that refused to relinquish the sixties?

WHEN SHE RETURNED to the farm, she found John in the same position as when she'd left. Head in his hands at the kitchen table that was littered with paper.

"Where the fuck are you?" he muttered to the ledger in front of him.

Phoebe dropped a kiss on his cheek and plunked the still cold lemonade down next to his elbow. "Problem, sexy farmer?"

"I'm missing $1.39," he muttered.

"Eeesh. Sounds serious."

"I've been looking and looking for the last goddamn hour. I can't find it."

She rattled her change purse. "I think I can spot you," she teased. His response was a grunt.

Phoebe peered over his shoulder. She tapped an entry. "Is that the entry from McCafferty's for the fence wire?" she asked.

He squinted at the page. "I don't know. I guess."

"You transposed the numbers," she said picking up the receipt at the top of the tower of disaster.

John snatched the receipt from her and glared at it and then the ledger. "Son of a bitch. I've been sitting here for hours!"

"Poor baby," Phoebe crooned, patting his head. "Are those mean old ledgers picking on you again?"

"How did you do that?" he asked, finally looking at her.

She shrugged and helped herself to a sip of his lemonade. "You may be a wordsmith, but I'm an accounting genius. I can help with the books. It's a sick fetish I have for numbers."

John shoved his chair back and got down on his knees on the worn linoleum. "I've changed my mind. I think we should get married."

Phoebe laughed and pretended to ignore the warmth that trickled into her belly.

He stood and lifted her up, swinging her in a circle. "Yep.

I've definitely fallen in love with your brain. How about a September wedding?"

"You're ridiculous," she said, linking her hands behind his neck as he let her slip to the floor. "In place of your terribly romantic proposal, I will accept a date with you tonight. Elvira invited us over for drinks—why doesn't Blue Moon have a bar, by the way? Michael will be there. And we ran into Hazel and invited her, too, to surprise Michael."

"Sounds good," he said, picking up the lemonade and taking a triumphant sip. "We can pick up pizza or subs on the way over. That new sub shop—what's it called?"

"Righteous Subs," Phoebe said, pulling a to-go menu from her back pocket. "I already have everyone's orders."

"Great minds," he said. She felt the levity between them shift just a bit as he eyed her over the menu.

"You look pretty today," he said suddenly and then looked down at the lemonade.

Self-consciously, Phoebe scooped her hair behind her ears. "So do you." She shook her head. "I mean, you look... good. Handsome. Sexy."

He put down the cup and slid his hands down her arms. "How much time do we have?"

"Enough," she breathed, sliding her hands under his shirt.

—————

19

*E*lvira's house was a tiny, salmon pink cottage on the outskirts of town. Her lot was large and wooded, making the one-story home look even smaller under the arching oaks and birch trees.

Phoebe and John followed the meandering sidewalk through hosta plants and ferns, past a grouping of mischievous gnomes dressed as The Beatles, to the covered front stoop.

"I think Pierce Acres needs a gnome," Phoebe said, slipping her arm through John's as he pressed the bell.

"I think a gnome is the last thing Pierce Acres needs," John said affably.

They heard footsteps from within, and Phoebe leaned in closer. "By the way, Elvira knows we slept together. Hi, El!"

She felt John tense beside her and jumped at the pinch he inflicted on her ass.

"Come on in. Hazel's already here. We're out back."

John held the door for Phoebe and Elvira pressed a wine glass into her hand. "Beer's in the fridge, John," Elvira said, leading the way through a postage stamp-sized living room with floor-to-ceiling bookcases bowing under their literary load.

There was a small fish tank with two colorful fish and a scuba diver that took up most of the sideboard in a dining room cozy enough to hold a table for four very good friends who didn't mind sitting on top of each other.

The kitchen was minuscule, but each inch of counter and cabinet were organized for efficiency.

Elvira, dressed in an off-the-shoulder gauze tunic and denim shorts, pushed through the screen door and Phoebe sighed with pleasure. The cottage's back deck had more square footage than the house itself. A beefy farmhouse table with seating for eight took up most of the top tier of the deck. Next to it, a cozy screened-in porch looked like the perfect place to spend a rainy day reading.

Strings of lights raced from the roof of the house out into the yard to the trunk of a massive oak and back again, bathing the yard in a soft glow.

The landscaping, more of everything, overflowed from large beds and made Phoebe think of the jungle. There were colorful pots of herbs and flowers scattered around the deck, a hammock tucked away in the corner of the yard, a fire pit, and a whimsical fountain.

"Wow, El. This is spectacular," Phoebe breathed.

"Home sweet home," Elvira said. "You good on wine, Hazel?" she called to the woman lounging on a chaise.

Hazel tilted her head in their direction. "Shh, I think I'm meditating."

"I heard you snore a minute ago. That's not meditating. That's napping," Elvira said, cheerfully topping off Hazel's glass.

"I got called in to the park at 3 a.m. this morning to help

Linus Fitzsimmons find the clothes he took off after drinking too much punch," she yawned.

Phoebe wondered what kind of a man little Billy would turn into with that kind of father.

"Anybody home?" Michael's voice carried from the front door back through the house.

"Out back," Elvira hollered. "I didn't tell him you were coming," she whispered conspiratorially to Hazel.

Michael, toting two six packs, waltzed through the back-door wearing a fitted Blue Moon Fire Department t-shirt and jeans. "Pierce, you forget where you keep your razor," he asked rubbing a hand over his own clean-shaven jaw.

Before John could fire back an insult, Michael spotted Hazel reclining like a goddess on her chair. He missed the step and went down hard.

John rescued one of the six-packs before it hit the deck and grinned.

"Oh, that was worth it," Elvira whispered to Phoebe. "You okay, there Michael?"

THEY PULLED up chairs around the chaise that Hazel had abandoned so Michael could elevate his swollen ankle. She'd even applied the first aid herself, wrapping his ankle in a snug Ace bandage and topping it with a bag of ice.

Phoebe leaned into John's side as everyone unwrapped their subs. "I think he literally just fell for her." She snickered at her own humor, and John gave her a dry look. "Oh, come on. That's funny."

"Debatable," John whispered back. "How's the ankle there, Cardona? You going to be able to climb a ladder to save any ferrets?" John opened a new beer for his friend.

Michael scoffed. "Please, this won't even slow down my six-minute mile." He said it while watching Hazel's face.

Hazel eyed him up. "Six flat?" she asked.

He shrugged. "Six thirty-two," he said with no small amount of pride.

"Huh, not bad," Hazel said, raising her fair eyebrows.

Phoebe could see it coming even before Michael did.

"Not bad? What do you run?" Michael leaned forward in the chaise, daring her to beat his time.

Hazel lifted her wine glass to her lips. "Six nineteen."

Michael called bullshit, and they immediately began planning a race to settle the dispute.

"They're going to be married and having babies in no time," Phoebe predicted.

"They've been dancing around each other for ten years. It's going to take more than a sprained ankle and Cardona's fat head to get those two out of their own ways," he predicted.

"What are you two whispering about over there?" Michael demanded. "Lovers' secrets?"

"Oooooh!" Elvira and Hazel made kissy noises reminiscent of twelve-year-old girls at a sleepover.

"I forgot to mention that Michael knows, too," Phoebe said in a stage whisper.

"You've got a big mouth," John told Phoebe.

She grinned guiltily. "Good news travels fast in Blue Moon." Which meant that, by tomorrow, most of the town would know that John was sleeping with his new farm hand. She hoped Mrs. Nordemann wouldn't take offense to pre-marital sex. Not that she and John were going to be marital.

John's bland tone snapped her out of her reverie. "Then I guess the entire town already knows Cardona here fell on his ass just looking at our sheriff friend."

"Oooooh!" Elvira and Phoebe crooned as Hazel sent Michael a long, questioning look. The tips of his ears turned pink again, something John didn't hesitate to point out to Hazel.

They ate and joked as the sky turned inky black and the stars popped out between the leaves of the trees. Hazel filled them in on some of her more amusing small town calls for aide. Elvira, her leg looped over the arm of her chair, filled them in on stories and scandals from Blue Moon's previous generation, and Phoebe answered questions about Penn State, sharing her impressive—and necessary—knowledge of the school's football program.

Elvira started a fire and turned on the radio in her kitchen, the blues—a neutral choice for Blue Moon, which was in a war between the '60s and '80s—poured through the window into the backyard. They lit citronella candles and incense sticks to chase away the mosquitos and broke into Elvira's stash of homemade ice cream.

John looped an arm over Phoebe's shoulders as Michael put everyone in stitches with a story about an English class substitute and Linus Fitzsimmons' special brownie recipe.

And right then, every damn thing in Phoebe's life was perfect.

WHEN ELVIRA GOT up to open another bottle of wine, she asked Phoebe and Hazel to come help her.

"Ooooh, girl talk," Michael called after them as they trooped inside.

Elvira held up two bottles. "Cab or blanc?"

Hazel and Phoebe pondered. "Blanc," they agreed.

Phoebe grabbed a bag of pretzels.

"Are you still hungry?" Hazel groaned stroking her flat stomach. "I ate my entire sub. All twelve inches of it."

"Twelve? Really, I wouldn't have expected Michael to have that kind of weaponry," Elvira teased.

Hazel grabbed a handful of pretzels from the bag and tossed them in Elvira's direction. "Hilarious."

"Soooo, what *is* going on with you and Michael?" Phoebe asked, leaning over the foot of countertop on the peninsula. Elvira joined her and stared expectantly.

"Yeah, Haze. What's going on with you and Fire Chief Hot Pants?"

"For a woman who doesn't want a relationship, you sure have a lot of interest in others'," Hazel said, pouring the sauvignon blanc.

"Just because I'm not getting married in this lifetime doesn't mean I don't do relationships. I do just fine in that department, thank you very much. Also, A HA! You said 'relationship' in relation to Michael."

Phoebe pointed at Elvira. "I believe the esteemed Ms. Eustace is correct."

Hazel rolled her blue eyes ceilingward. "Are you sure you weren't born to some hippies here in town and adopted? I feel like I'm trapped in a room with Nordemann right now."

"I hate to point it out, but you're avoiding the question," Phoebe grinned. "There's something there, right?"

"Ugh, fine. I may have had the smallest crush on him in high school, but the way he asked me to prom? All big man on campus?" Hazel snorted. "I want a regular guy, not Mr. I'm God's Gift to Women."

"He is a flirt," Elvira agreed.

"But he clearly has a thing for you," Phoebe argued.

"See? What did I tell you? Nordemann," Hazel said, slipping her hand in the pretzel bag.

"I'm serious. The man just fell on his ass just because he caught a glimpse of you," Phoebe reminded her.

"Hmm."

"Yeah, but how is Hazel supposed to ignore his long history of womanizing?"

Phoebe waved away Elvira's concern. "Please, long, *ancient* history."

"He asked you out, didn't he?" Elvira reminded Phoebe.

"To annoy John. Besides, the first time I saw him look at Hazel at the town meeting, I knew there were sparks aplenty."

"So, one night of sex turns you into a relationship expert?" Hazel questioned.

"Correction, one night of phenomenally mind-blowing sex. And, Exhibit B," she waved her hand in front of her face. "I'm not blind. Anyone can see Michael has a very heavy thing for you."

"Having a thing for and behaving as a partner in a monogamous relationship are two very different things," Elvira pointed out, holding up her empty glass.

Hazel poured obligingly. "And do I even want to be the thousandth notch in his bed post?" Hazel argued.

"Hazel, if anyone can lay down the law with Cardona, it's you," Phoebe predicted.

Hazel poured. "I see what you're doing. Good cop, bad cop. It doesn't work on an actual cop."

Phoebe grinned. "Just giving you some food for thought."

"You sure you aren't moving here permanently?" Hazel asked Phoebe. "You'd fit right in with the rest of these gossip mongers and meddlers."

"Phoebe's got some family stuff to take care of after this summer," Elvira announced vaguely.

Phoebe shot her a look.

"Uh-uh." Hazel shook her finger in Phoebe's face. "I

shared, now you. Or I'll dig my service weapon out of my purse and interrogate you properly."

Elvira snickered. "When's the last time you had to interrogate anyone?"

"When two of those punk-ass Karlinski kids took Carson's tractor for a joy ride through downtown before parking it in the creek. And back to Phoebe." Hazel pointed pistol fingers in her direction.

"Stupid town and stupid people wanting to know everything," Phoebe muttered.

"Yeah, not so fun now is it, smarty pants?" Hazel's grin was sharp. "Spill it, sister."

So Phoebe did over another glass of wine and more pretzels.

"Well, that sucks. What about you and Farmer Gorgeous out there?" Hazel nodded toward the backyard.

"We're just temporary. Monogamous but temporary," she explained.

"You look pretty sad when you say that," Elvira prodded, her chin in her hand.

Phoebe wrinkled her nose. "I don't know. I think maybe there's something in the water in this town. I'm actually not looking forward to leaving."

She didn't miss the long look that passed between Elvira and Hazel.

"What?" she demanded.

"Nothing, geez. Suspicious much?" Hazel covered.

"You're still going to be in town for the Sit-In, right?" Elvira asked, glancing at the kitten calendar on the front of her refrigerator.

"The Sit-In?"

Hazel and Elvira shared another look. "Oh, you can't miss the Sit-In," Hazel grinned.

"What are you protesting?"

"Nothing," Elvira laughed. "It's the anniversary of this one time that the town protested something—"

"The library closing," Hazel supplied.

"Right, right. Anyway, our sleepy little hippie town hit the news that night for the protest staged at the library. People showed up, hats were passed, and the library stayed open."

"As the years went on, there weren't as many things to protest here. So it's more of a carnival," Elvira explained. "With handcuffs."

"Handcuffs?" Phoebe blinked.

"It's part of the tradition. And we still raise money, though," Hazel continued. "A different cause every year."

"What's this year's cause," Phoebe asked. *God, what a sweet, kooky little town. It was going to tear a piece of her heart out to leave this ridiculous place.*

"As far as I know," Hazel said breezily, "Mayor Nordemann hasn't announced it yet. We're not exactly good at planning around here."

20

*P*hoebe and John let nature take its course in the fields and the bedroom. Long, sweaty days of satisfying work were followed by cool showers and hot nights. The rough edges of Phoebe's thesis were smoothed out with careful edits as the calluses on her palms hardened from the labor. John took her wading in the creek, picnicking in the fields, and showed her the spot he'd chosen for a pond someday.

She could see it. She could tell John was imagining a family cooling off on hot summer nights in the water. His family. He wanted it, and he'd have it someday soon, she guessed. At least once she was out of his way.

John Pierce was a man who knew what he wanted, and she admired that about him. It made her question some of her own goals. What did she really want beyond settling her parents' debt? She'd pursued this major because she'd loved those years on her grandparents' farm. Would settling into the research community really fulfill her?

She'd had an unsettling moment the other night when she and John enjoyed fresh squeezed lemonade on the front porch and debated where he should hang a porch swing. For just a second, she wished that she'd still be here when he hung the swing.

She'd shaken it off and distracted herself by distracting John with an entertaining strip dance on the porch. They'd barely made it inside. He was going to have to burn down the house if he didn't want a wife facing down memories of Phoebe here.

She was everywhere here. Phoebe cooked while John cleaned up, they wrote together—John still refusing to share with her anything he'd written—and every night they made love until they fell asleep entwined. One day, they went to town for a "few things" and returned with utensils, a casserole dish, new towels, and a second set of sheets. Not that they needed them. Phoebe slept in his bed every night, the sheets usually landing in a tangle on the floor. When John shored up the sagging porch roof, Phoebe weeded and mulched the overgrown flower beds at the front of the house, taking the house from dilapidated to charming.

They made a good team, Phoebe decided.

They'd gone from argumentative foes to lovers in sync, and it felt... good.

Phoebe swiped an arm over her brow, transferring sweat to sweat. The humidity clung to the pasture like a wet wool blanket. Heavy and oppressive. The air felt like it was too thick to breathe. But that didn't stop John from working at full speed.

They'd built a shelter in the pasture. A place for Melanie to enjoy the shade or stay out of the rain.

At the distant rumble of thunder, Phoebe dropped the paintbrush in the tray and sat on her haunches admiring the view. John, stripped to the waist, hefted a piece of lumber and tossed it into the back of the pick-up. Sweat slicked his bronze skin, trickling over ridges of muscle and disappearing into the loose waistband of his jeans. The denim rode indecently low on his hips.

Dark, swollen clouds roiled behind him. He looked like a sexy, brooding hero of one of those supermarket paperbacks. If he were on the cover of a book, Phoebe would be compelled to buy it.

As if reading her thoughts, he lifted his gaze to her. He stripped off his work gloves and tossed them in the bed of the truck. "You're quiet," he said, taking the cup of water she offered him from the thermos.

"Just enjoying the scenery," she grinned.

His heated gaze was punctuated by the next roll of thunder. With that hint of danger, Phoebe felt her heart stutter.

She wasn't sure if it was the heat from the hazy sun overhead or the look in John's eyes that made her feel like she was baking in a convection oven. The wind, hot and thick, picked up, and the tips of grass in the pasture swirled in wild patterns.

"Storm's coming," John said, eyeing the growing clouds.

She could smell it, that metallic hint of rain on the wind. In the distance, lightning flashed in the clouds, and Phoebe felt the hair on her arms stand up. "Maybe we should call it a day?"

"Probably a good idea," he agreed. His tone was mild, but she could see that heat in his eyes and knew what he was thinking. They'd spent so little time together, but opening up to the kind of intimacy they shared in bed made her feel like she knew the man down to his bones. And the way he was looking at her now had Phoebe thinking of things besides cool showers and fresh iced-tea.

Lightning forked across the sky, chased by a long rumble of thunder that went on forever.

John gave her a light shove toward the truck. "Get in," he ordered.

He loaded up the paint supplies and tools into the bed and climbed in behind the wheel just as the first, fat drops fell from the sky. Within seconds the drops turned to an honest to goodness downpour so heavy Phoebe hoped it wouldn't crack the windshield.

John drove by feel, sticking to the tire ruts in the trail that had taken them out of sight of civilization. The storm was upon them, turning the trail into a river of mud, at least from what little Phoebe could see between paltry swipes of the windshield wipers. But she wasn't worried. There wasn't a person alive who knew this land better than John.

She caught the flash of red from the barn ahead and knew that there, through the distorted glass, was the dry sanctuary of home.

John pulled into the three-sided shelter that housed the truck and tractor on the far side of the house.

"Gonna have to make a run for it. You ready?"

"A little rain doesn't scare me," Phoebe scoffed.

"Let's see those long legs in action," John winked.

Their mad dash was more slip and slide than sprint. The dirt and gravel drive was a muddy lake. She felt it, warm and wet, coating her calves as she ran.

They left a watery, mud-laden trail up the front steps. Phoebe pushed her wet hair out of her eyes and levered off her boots next to the door. Her grimy white t-shirt was plastered to her, and she felt John watching her. It was an adrenaline rush, that untamed lust in those gray eyes gone molten.

The rain impacted the porch roof, streaming over the gutters in an endless torrent.

Teasing them both, Phoebe straightened, sliding her thumbs into the waistband of her jeans. She undid her fly with uncharacteristic leisure and slowly wriggled out of the wet denim.

John, muscled jaw tight now, toed off his work books, kicking them aside.

She reached for the hem of her t-shirt but got no further. He was on her, big hands lifting her up, settling her on his hips, wrapping her legs around him.

He tasted of salt and smelled like storm, a heady combination that aroused her. He was all man. Every inch of ripped muscle, every callus, every move of his powerful body. She couldn't imagine a more potent aphrodisiac than the man she was wrapped around.

In the next weak breath, they were through the door and stumbling up the stairs as lightning lit the prematurely darkened house from outside.

John kicked the bedroom door open with gusto and dropped them both on the bed, the mattress springs protesting. Flailing wildly, he yanked her shirt over her head with one hand and snapped on the bedside lamp with the other.

She'd had him in nearly every way possible, Phoebe thought, tugging off his shirt and running her hungry hands down his back. Slow and sweet in the early dawn, languidly, teasingly in the late afternoons or after midnight. He took his time every time with her. But this desperation, this raw intensity was new and beautiful.

Her body yearned for his. She hitched her legs higher up his hips, and he pressed himself against her. Damp, rigid denim grinded against the cotton of her briefs. He used one hand to unzip his fly, and Phoebe eagerly shoved at his jeans with her heels.

She needed him closer. He kissed her feverishly, and for a moment she forgot everything she'd ever known. Everything she'd ever dreamed or wanted or accomplished. All that mattered was right here, right now. He made her feel like this fragile thing ready to be worshipped by mouth and hands. It made her dizzy.

Another bolt of lightning lit the sky through the windows, and the lamp went out with a snap. The thunder reverberated in her bones. The storm had robbed the house of power but not them. They still had all they needed.

Phoebe used her legs to kick and roll, pinning John to his back. The sheet fell to the floor. The rain pounded against the panes of glass. And John's sterling eyes held her under an unspoken spell. Together, they worked his boxers off and then her underwear, and as his big, hard hands roamed her body, Phoebe made a grab for the box of condoms that had taken up residence on the nightstand.

"Tell me what you want," she whispered.

"I want to give you what you want."

His whispered confession, rasped between rolls of thunder gave her goose bumps on every inch of her skin.

"I want you to *take*." He always gave and gave and gave until she was loose and nearly comatose. And, for once, she wanted to watch him take just for himself. To be greedy with her body. She wanted to see him selfish and craving, using her body to take him over that jagged edge of desire.

She slid her hand down across taut abs, stroking down one thigh and up the other. Her fingertips burned from the heat pumping off him.

Unable to wait any longer, Phoebe gripped his thick shaft and leaned forward to taste him. She knew how to get him to the point where he was delirious with the need to take, to consume.

"Phoebe," he hissed out her name.

"It's okay," she promised and took him into her mouth. She could tell by the rigid muscle under her hands that John was using every ounce of strength to stay perfectly still for her. But she would break him down.

Slicking down over him again and again, Phoebe followed her mouth with the grip of her hand. She'd let him pleasure her so often these past few weeks, but that didn't mean she hadn't been learning his body, his cues.

He groaned as if tormented by her pleasure, and she lapped at him with the flat of her tongue drawing a strangled "fuck" from his lips.

When he could take her torture no more, John clamped a hand over her wrist. "You need to stop. Now."

She obeyed but only to roll the condom onto his straining shaft. Just that perfunctory touch had John's hips levering off the bed, his body begging for more.

Before he could regain any control, Phoebe moved to straddle his hips and, in one swift move, took him inside her. They gasped together at the invasion, so sensual, so shocking. Phoebe felt it, that biological relief at being possessed by John.

It was nothing she'd ever sought out or wanted—not that she'd known such a feeling existed—but Phoebe couldn't pretend that the raw vulnerability he made her feel wasn't real. Making love to John was nothing like any of her previous, limited experience. There was something here that went beyond pleasure and beyond scratching an itch.

John came to life under her, his hands cupping her breasts, kneading her flesh and sending shocks of pleasure through her straining nipples.

She rose on her knees only to sink down on him again, sheathing his cock within her. She wasn't sure how much of her own torture she could take before she gave in to the cravings that screamed through her blood. She wanted to drive John past his tenderness, his care-taking. She wanted to push him into the dark, delicious desire that he so often held her captive in.

She leaned down, the tips of her breasts dragging across his chest, and when she took his mouth, he wrestled control from her. He withdrew abruptly and her muscles clenched weakly around the emptiness. And then he was on his knees behind her, lifting her hips.

Phoebe buried her face in the lone pillow left on the bed. It smelled like him. He guided her hips higher and then drove into her with a ferocity that had her gasping for breath.

"Too much?" he gritted out, barely slowing his pace.

It took her a moment to find the word, to catch her breath. "More!"

Her demand was met with a soft grunt as he used her hips to thrust into her harder than he'd ever taken her.

"Is this what you want?" he demanded, on a low growl.

"God, yes!"

He released one hip and gripped her breast that reverberated with every thrust.

She'd wanted this, but she had no idea where it would take them. She was a prisoner of John's pleasure, and it overwhelmed her.

He was riding her recklessly as if racing toward a finish that only he could see. The primal need for release built within her until she quivered around his shaft. It was too much. Phoebe feared her body would break apart into pieces, slivers of pleasure.

His shout, triumphant and desperate, echoed in her ears, and as he came, he reached between her legs, stroking her over the edge. She joined him, careening into the lightning and wind as her body shook with each wrenching wave.

~

"WHAT. THE. HELL. WAS. THAT?" John's breathing was still ragged from the orgasm that had ripped him to pieces.

Phoebe laughed or coughed under him. He couldn't tell with her face pressed into the pillow.

He hoped she wasn't suffocating because he really didn't have the energy to roll off of her at the moment. He was still inside her, still feeling the aftershocks of her own release around his half-hard cock.

"I just need a minute," he murmured against the smooth skin of her back. "An hour tops."

There was still no discernible response from Phoebe, and he worried that she might have already suffocated. With effort, he slid over onto his side and pulled Phoebe's face out of the pillow.

"You still breathing?"

"Mmm." Without opening her eyes, she rolled and snuggled into his chest, a smug smile on her pretty face.

A wave of feeling swamped him as he pressed his face to her damp hair. *He'd been wrong, dead wrong.* And that rarely happened. He was a planner, a weigh-er, a debater. His decisions were rational and well thought-out. Yet, with that approach, he would have missed out on the woman cradled against his chest.

They didn't make sense together, but what they did make was a hell of a lot more addicting than logic.

John had known the satisfaction at the end of a hard day's work. Felt the joy of time spent with loved ones, the pride in the harvest of a crop grown by his own two hands. He'd enjoyed the carnal delights that sex had to offer.

But nothing in his life prepared him for what he felt in bed with Phoebe. Every time he came, it was as if he emptied himself into her only to be refilled with... what was it? That strange glow. Well-being, satisfaction, peace? He couldn't put a finger on it. But it was warm and bright and flooded him.

Fuck. Was this love? Is that what was glowing in his chest for Phoebe?

The twitch in his eye was back.

Why couldn't he be more like Cardona? A sexual connoisseur with a passing enjoyment of the buffet of women. No, he had to fall in love with the woman he couldn't keep for longer than a summer, a season.

21

*P*hoebe unwrapped herself from the phone cord and hung up dancing a jig. John looked up blandly from his papers. "And how's Elvira?" he asked.

Phoebe knew it was a perfunctory question as he'd heard every word of her end of the conversation. She danced over to him and leaned over his shoulder.

Reflexively, he covered his writing, and Phoebe gave him a little pinch.

"El had some news."

"I gathered that from all the 'no ways' and 'are you kidding mes'," he said dryly.

"Well, then smarty pants. What's the news?" Phoebe flopped down in the chair closest to his.

"Cardona asked out Hazel," John guessed.

Phoebe felt herself deflate. "How did you know?"

"He told me he was going to."

"And you didn't tell me?" Phoebe slapped at his arm. "Honestly, John. Sometimes I think *I* was the one who was supposed to be born in Blue Moon."

He grinned at her and pulled her chair closer to him until he could reach her for a kiss.

"Well?" she asked, pulling back.

"Well, what?"

"What do you think?"

"About what?"

"Michael and Hazel?"

"I'm a lot more interested in you and me," he told her with a devilish smile. He brought her finger tips to his mouth and nipped one.

"You know, for someone who was so resistant to going to bed with me, you certainly are making up for lost time," she reminded him with a saucy wink.

Dinner was over, the dishes were done, Murdock was snoring under the table. Before the phone call, Phoebe had been putting another round of "finishing touches" on her thesis while John scratched at his own writing project.

It was their own time, and Phoebe had grown to enjoy these nights spent in companionable quiet. Of course, a TV would have been nice, too.

She sighed.

"What's that for?" John asked.

"Oh, I don't know," she said airily. "Life is pretty good. There's really only one thing that I want. One thing that I need."

Phoebe enjoyed how his gaze heated at just the idea of sex.

"And what's that one thing?" he asked, kissing the inside of her wrist and sending a delicious shiver down her spine.

"I want to read something you wrote." Her declaration had the same effect as dumping a bucket of freezing creek water over his head. John leaned back in his chair and groaned. He covered his face in his hands.

"You drive me insane," he announced through his palms.

Phoebe grinned unapologetically. "I know. So you might as well just hand something over now. It'll be easier in the long run."

He shoved a stack of papers at her. "Read *one*. And do not comment on it. I don't do this for other people's opinions. I do it for me," he reminded her.

Phoebe bounced up and down in her chair. "Oh, boy!"

She started at the top of the stack knowing if she took her time digging through the papers, it would just upset John more. Wiggling to get comfortable in her seat, Phoebe cleared her throat.

"No! Not out loud. Christ, I can't be here when you read it," John said, shoving his chair back from the table. "I'll be back in five minutes." He picked up his beer, whistled for the dog, and left through the side door.

Phoebe, bubbling with glee, settled in to read.

Visions of future passing

When I look at this land, I know it's not the present that I see. I don't see a dilapidated barn that's about to fall or a farmhouse that desperately needs an overhaul. I don't see broken fence lines and overgrown fields.

I see the future. That red barn painted up nice with white trim. Horses in the stalls and pastures. Kids spending an endless summer splashing in the pond. Lightning bugs dotting the fields and shooting stars streaking across an inky black sky.

I see acres of corn and wheat and soy. Fields of tomatoes, beans, squash, lettuce, berries. I see family and friends and bonfires after hard, gratifying days of work. I catch glimpses of long winters buried under feet of snow. A fire crackling in the hearth and stew simmering on the stove. Snowball fights and snowmen. *Christmas trees with lights. Dark nights warm under a quilt as snow falls softly outside.*

I can taste the apple cider and beer and burgers on the grill and pies fresh from the oven. Hear the laughter. Children at play, wild and free. A wife at night, quiet and teasing.

I see community. A town that never gives up on anyone. One that butts in even when it's not wanted. Neighbors that show up to help without being asked because they know you and love you.

From this vantage point, I can see for miles into the future. There will be growth here. There will be family here. Harvests here. Happiness here.

I can hear it, too.

The high school marching band warming up before a football game.

The crickets on a summer night.

"Just five more minutes, dad."

"I love you, John."

There is something that I can find here and only here on these two hundred acres. I feel it in my bones as if they're made from the same ground beneath my boots. I'm meant to be here, meant to work this earth. I'm meant to live here, love here, die here.

Phoebe loosened her grip on the papers in her hand, her eyes damp, her chest tight. He'd painted a picture of a beautiful, perfect life. He was a poet, a man who would be a hero to his wife and children.

The hairs on her arms stood up as if lightning were about to strike. Perhaps it already had. Not outside in the dark where man and dog wandered. But in her chest where her heart beat for the man who'd written down the life he wanted in blue ink on lined paper.

She'd gone and done it. She'd let down her guard and fallen in love with John Pierce, poet farmer.

22

*P*hoebe refilled the kibble in Murdock's food dish and opened the door to welcome the rain-cooled breeze. After last night's storm, they hadn't been expecting more rain, but the heavens had opened up again for a brief but satisfying drenching which ended their day a little early.

Phoebe laughed watching the little dog wag his stump of a tail as he chewed. She could hear John singing Culture Club upstairs in the shower, and it brought a smile to her lips.

It seemed like all the occupants of Pierce Acres were feeling the mood. She felt lighter than she had since her father's accident. This moment, this day, this summer was turning out to be so much more than she could have hoped for.

She grabbed the chicken breasts that she'd been marinating in the refrigerator and turned on the oven. She'd pair the chicken with light salads and John's own green beans fresh from the garden.

Humming, Phoebe slid the chicken into the new casserole dish. Her first impression of John as the hero, the caretaker, had proven to be correct. All she needed to do was mention how a casserole dish would open up her menu offerings or tell him about her grandmother's sourdough waffle recipe, and within days, a cheerful red dish and new waffle iron made their way into the kitchen.

The phone on the kitchen wall rang, and Phoebe kicked the oven door shut, wiped her hands on the tea towel on the counter, and picked up the phone.

"Pierce residence," she said cheerily.

"Hi, sweetheart!" Phoebe could hear the excitement in her mother's breathless greeting.

"Hi, Mom. How are—"

"I just got off the phone with a Mr.—" Phoebe heard papers rustling on her mother's end. "Ingersol with the FDA."

Phoebe's hand tightened on the orange receiver. "What did he say?" Her voice rose seven octaves. Murdock shot her a wary look before going back to his food.

JOHN PADDED DOWNSTAIRS BAREFOOT, hair still damp from his shower. He heard Phoebe in the kitchen. Her voice happy, her laughter bright. It was hard to remember what the house had been like before her. Quiet. Very quiet, he decided.

The phone cord stretched across the doorway. The meager foot-long cord had been plenty for him. To John, phone calls should be brief, perfunctory. But to Phoebe, they were a way to give detailed reports of every second of her week to her parents, her sister, and friends. His long-distance bill was going to be astronomical.

"A job? You're sure he said they were offering me a job?" Phoebe asked, squealing a moment later. "Mom, this is everything that we need!"

He didn't mean to eavesdrop, John told himself. Technically, it was his house. And technically, he was just standing in the hallway where Phoebe could see him if she walked past the doorway. It wasn't like he was hiding.

She crossed the doorway. One hand on her head, her smile bright, her gaze on the ceiling, and he ducked behind the old hutch in the hallway. "Yes, of course this is what I want, Mom. Why do you think I would change my mind?"

A job with the FDA. It's exactly what she'd wanted, what she'd planned for. Then why didn't he feel happy for her? Why did he feel like his stomach had just dropped into an elevator shaft? He faced the wall, staring at the hideous black and orange wallpaper. It was on his list. This whole fucking house was on his list.

Why would she want to stay in a broken-down place with ten seconds of hot water and shitty orange flowers peeling off the wall? She knew what she wanted. A good job in a flashy city with a paycheck flush enough to support her parents. It was a shame that he knew what he wanted now, too. Phoebe. But he couldn't give her what she wanted.

"Don't cry, Mom. Please?" Phoebe's voice was softer now. "You and Dad sacrificed for the last twenty plus years for me and Rose. It's our turn, and you'll be back on your feet and planning cruises and dinner parties in no time."

She was quiet for a moment or two, and John could feel her enthusiasm fade just a bit. "I promise this is what I want, Mom. My thesis is almost done. I've been polishing it for a while."

She paced past the doorway again, staring straight ahead. The smile was gone.

"I'll call him back first thing in the morning and let you know what happens, okay?"

John kicked at the dusty wall trim and, for the first time ever, regretted his choices.

"I love you, too, Mom. Give my love to Dad."

PHOEBE WOLFED down her scrambled eggs and bacon, focusing on the tasks ahead of her for the day. There was the back-breaking, never-ending harvest of zucchini and cucumbers, another coat of paint on the west side of the barn, watering the flower beds, weeding for the zillionth time, and, oh yeah, telling John she had a day to accept a position as a research assistant with the FDA.

Starting in two weeks. In Washington, D.C.

She should be thrilled, ecstatic even. This was the outcome she'd been praying for. And yet she hadn't been able to say yes to the very dry, very business-like Mr. Ingersol.

She'd almost brought it up at dinner last night, but John had been unusually quiet. His one- and two-word answers had been few and far between. She hoped he wasn't coming down with a summer cold. There was so much to do before she left. So much time she wanted to spend with him.

John walked into the kitchen, studiously avoiding her gaze. He poured his coffee and snatched a strip of bacon off the plate next to the stove.

So much had changed this summer. And one of those things seemed to be her dreams for the future. Phoebe hadn't been prepared for this shift. She wasn't even sure this was real. She'd never been in love before.

She'd lain awake last night for hours thinking about John's essay on Pierce Acres. No, not just thinking, she corrected herself. She could *see* it as if she were there.

School delays on snow days, Thanksgiving dinners, lazy Sunday afternoons with locusts buzzing in the background and the summer sun coaxing the fields to their full production.

Children and pets and farm animals. Neighbors and friends. Family crowding around the dining room table, which would have chairs by then. What spell had John woven with his words that his future had become her dream? She wasn't ready for marriage, children, settling down. *Was she?*

She didn't know. And she needed some time to think. If she could find another way to get the money for her parents, maybe a job in D.C. didn't have to be the only answer.

"Morning," she said, hoping to distract herself with conversation.

John faced her without looking her in the eyes. He had papers in his hand.

He crossed to her, handed them over, and walked back to the stove.

"What's this?" she asked.

"Your thesis. It's done."

"You liked it?" She was relieved. It was his second full read-through and her nine millionth draft. John's opinion carried weight with her, and if he was happy with her hours of labor, then maybe her professors would be, too.

"I don't have a doctorate, but I think you make your points clearly and succinctly."

She let out a slow breath, her hands rubbing her eyes. "You have no idea how relieved I am to hear that. I've been working on it for so long I was starting to think it was completely shit."

"It's not. But what is shit is you wasting your time here, Phoebe. Your paper doesn't need polishing. It needs to be turned in." His tone was flat, his eyes dark.

"There are still some areas I want to work on," she argued. There was some data she wanted to cross-reference, some points she wanted to shore up. A man she wasn't ready to leave.

But he was shaking his head. "Why are you putting it off?"

"I'm not!"

"You have a perfect, finished thesis. You could have your master's degree in hand. Why are you sitting at my table?"

"Are you kidding me right now?" she asked.

He met her gaze coolly. "You're wasting your time here."

"We have an agreement. You help me with my thesis. I help you for the summer. Just because one's done doesn't mean the other's done, too." She pushed away from the table and rinsed her mug in the sink. "You're being ridiculous right now. I'll see you out in the fields after you've had more coffee and start making sense again."

But before she could make it to the door, he had her by the arm and was towing her backwards.

"I'm serious, Phoebe. I think you should go. Today."

She shook her head, certain she was misunderstanding him somehow. "John, no. We're in the middle of picking squash, and I'm making burgers tonight. Elvira's coming over tomorrow—"

"There's no point in you staying here prolonging the inevitable. You're leaving. It might as well be now."

"Who's going to help you?" she demanded, pointing toward the fields.

"I got along just fine without you before you showed up here. I'm sure I can fumble my way through the harvest."

Tears inexplicably welled in her eyes. She'd earned her place here. She was valuable to him. Damn it, she had more to give him before she had to go.

"Go spend time with your family before you start your job."

"How did you know—"

"I heard you on the phone last night. You should have told me." At least there was a hint of something besides disinterest now in his voice.

"I was going to. I hadn't decided..."

"You haven't decided what?" John shoved a hand through his dark hair. "To take it? That's bullshit. This is exactly what you wanted. You'd be stupid to turn down an opportunity like this."

"Maybe I was hoping for another opportunity," she shot back.

"Like what exactly?" The condescension in John's tone was heavy enough that Phoebe didn't feel the need to respond.

"I don't know. I have time before I have to decide." Twenty-three hours and forty minutes to be exact.

"It's what you want. Don't start questioning it now."

"Don't you want me to stay?" The words burned a trail up her throat and then hung in the air between them.

She saw the flash in the depths of his eyes, felt the reflexive tightening of his fingers on her arm just before the lie.

"No."

"John." She was moving from hurt to pissed the fuck off with alarming speed. "Don't pretend like I don't mean anything to you."

"Don't pretend like we have a future," he countered. "What we had was... fun. But it's over. There's no reason for you to stay."

"You're an idiot," she snapped. Phoebe wrenched free from his grip. "I guess I have some packing to do."

She stormed out of the kitchen with her heart in pieces.

23

"This is everything," Phoebe said, swiping her palms over the seat of her jeans. Her bags that she'd reluctantly packed while wiping away tears, sat at her feet.

He was supposed to call her bluff now. Faced with a Phoebe-less life, he was supposed to come to his senses and beg her to stay.

John nodded and took her suitcase for her. "I'll carry this out for you."

Was he in that big of a hurry to get rid of her? Phoebe wondered. *Didn't he see that her heart was breaking? Or did he see and not care?*

She followed him out the front door, her heart shattering with every single step. She crossed the front porch that she'd miss so much, the rickety steps that kept getting pushed further and further down the fix list. He'd pulled her car around for her as if to hurry her along.

How could he not care? After all those nights drowning in each other, pleasing each other, worshipping each other. How could it just end?

All he needed to do was ask her to stay. One little word. "Stay." And maybe three more words. "I'm an idiot."

But he was loading her suitcase into the trunk of her Triumph and then taking her typewriter and loading it, too.

John shoved his hands in his pockets, shoulders hunched, his expression unreadable.

"Well, I guess this is it," Phoebe began, staring down at the dirt and stone of the drive under her sandals.

"Guess so," he said. His face was stoic, not a hint of emotion. He could have been watching a golf tournament on TV instead of saying goodbye to the woman whose life he'd changed.

It wasn't fair. She was eviscerated, and he was fine. Absolutely fine. Just another day to him. He was probably excited to get his life back. He and Murdock could enjoy the peace and quiet of the farm without her.

She, on the other hand, would turn into a hysterical blubbering mess every time she smelled hay and sunshine. Memories of John Pierce haunting her forever.

"Thanks for... everything," she said. Her voice quivered, and she wanted to punch herself in the face. If he wanted to do this the emotionless way, who was she to make a scene?

Oh, fuck it all.

"Damnit, John. Ask me to stay!" She shoved at his chest with the flat of her hand.

His jaw clenched at her demand. But the twitch at his eye, the one that appeared when she'd pushed him past his breaking point, was absent.

"I can't do that, Phoebe."

"Why the hell not?"

"You know why not," he snapped the words out. "You have a job lined up, you have plans, you have a family to support. You can't do any of that from here."

"Help me find a way." She hated herself for begging. Hated herself for wanting him to offer a solution. "Please. Help me, John."

"There's no way, Phoebe."

All softness was gone. This was a perfunctory goodbye. If he'd cared, he would have tried harder... or at all.

She cleared her throat, trying to reassemble the pieces of her dignity.

"Nice knowing you," she snapped out and climbed behind the wheel.

"Phoebe." His hand gripped her door.

Finally, she breathed.

"Drive safely."

She almost flipped him the bird, barely resisted the urge as she eased down the drive toward the road. After everything that had happened, she'd been the one to fall, and that son of a bitch had broken her heart. She hoped his farm burned down and he had to move in with the Nordemanns.

Phoebe headed east instead of west not paying attention to the landscape that blurred through her window. She wasn't in any shape to see the town she'd fallen hard for one last time. Blue Moon Bend would always be home to her, even if she never saw it again. She rounded a curve and broke through the wide swath of woods and slammed on the brakes.

This was still John's land. She was sure of it. The field he'd told her he was leaving fallow was no longer empty. In it bloomed thousands and thousands of sunflowers, reaching their lemon-yellow faces toward the sun. Soft green leaves, giant dark centers. They stretched on forever, staring at her, leaves waving gently in the breeze.

It was the most beautiful sight she'd ever seen. And that asshole had planted them for her. He'd planted her a field of sunflowers and *still* let her go pretending that he didn't love her.

She maneuvered a sloppy three-point turn on the skinny ribbon of road and headed back to heartache. She plowed down the driveway and braked in a cloud of dust.

John was sitting on the front porch steps, his head in his hands.

Phoebe hopped out and slammed the door hard enough to make the car shake. "Do you even *know* that you love me?"

John lifted his head out of his hands and stared dumbfounded.

"Hello?" she waved her hand in front of his face. "You planted me acres of sunflowers because they're my favorite, and yet you send me off without even a 'nice knowing you'? That's a dick move, John."

"You're back?" he whispered.

"I'm back here to tell you you're an idiot. You love me. I love you. And you still don't even want to try to make this work."

"You love me?" He rose, and she took a step back, wondering if she'd made a mistake. But she was already committed to a tirade.

"Yeah, I love you, you gigantic idiot."

He grabbed her. Hard. And pulled her into his arms. "I changed my mind."

Her face was flattened against his chest, and try as she might, she couldn't wriggle her way free. "Changed your mind about what?" she asked, her voice muffled by his spectacular pectorals.

"I can't let you go. I thought I could. I thought it was best for your family. We'll just have to think of something else. Maybe they can move in here with us until they get back on their feet? Or maybe they'll want to stay when we have kids. Family's important."

"What?" Her head was spinning.

"We'll figure it out. But you're staying," he fumbled through her pockets and grabbed her car keys out of her jeans. "I don't care how good that job is. You won't love it like you'll learn to love me." He pitched the keys over his shoulder, and they landed in a flowerbed.

"What are you—"

But his mouth was on hers with a desperation she'd never known in him. Patient, tender, demanding, yes. But he was kissing her like he was breathing her life into his body. And the way her knees buckled, she guessed he'd achieved his goal.

His tongue licked into her mouth, and she tasted him. That flavor that she thought she'd go her entire life without ever experiencing again lit her up, scorching her from the inside out.

She had to breathe, had to get her bearings.

"Mmm, John. John!" She had to give him a hard shove to get him to break the kiss. "I don't understand what you're telling me."

"I'm telling you we're getting married and your parents are moving in with us. I'll get a second job if I need to. A third one, too. But you're not going. I'm sorry. It's a great opportunity. But you have to stay."

Murdock yipped in agreement at her heels.

"We're getting married?" She couldn't think without an ounce of blood in her brain.

"Of course, we are. How's this weekend for you?"

"This weekend?" She was repeating everything he said like she'd lost her damn mind. And maybe she had. But so had John.

"I love you, Phoebe." He pressed his mouth to hers again, and she finally started to understand. His hands, so big and strong baring the scars of hard work, stroked up her sides under the edge of her tank top and her legs turned to Jell-O.

"Say it back," he breathed, dropping kisses on her mouth and cheeks.

"I love you, Phoebe," she sighed.

He pinched her and she managed a weak laugh. "I love you, John. And this weekend is just fine for me. But what about our parents? Won't they want to see us get married?"

"Mine are easy. They've been talking about coming back for a visit soon anyway. But someone's going to have to break the news to your father that you broke up my marriage to Elvira."

Phoebe clapped a hand to her forehead. "Maybe we don't need to tell our parents."

The phone in the house rang.

"Ignore it. It's been ringing for the past ten minutes."

"It might be something important," Phoebe scolded him.

"This is important," he said, lifting her up and wrapping her legs around his waist. "This is the only important thing."

She heard the car coming down the drive and then another one and another one. "Are you throwing a party?" she demanded.

John spun, his hands splayed across her ass. "What in the hell is this?"

Elvira, Michael, and Hazel jumped out of the first car. "Phoebe!" Elvira jogged up, her face flushed and happy.

More car doors slammed and Mooners flooded the yard.

"You all missed the Sit-In!" Mrs. Nordemann huffed and puffed, dragging the elusive Mr. Nordemann along behind her.

"You were supposed to be the guest of honor," Bruce

Oakleigh said, crossing his arms over the drum kit he wore around his waist. Phoebe wondered how he got in the car wearing it.

"We like totally had a surprise for you," Rainbow said, cracking her gum.

Reluctantly, John released Phoebe, setting her on the ground.

"Guys, we're kind of busy right now," he began. "We're planning a wedding."

"We all better be invited," Mrs. Nordemann announced, putting a finger in his face. "Hazel!" She waved the sheriff over. "Do the honors, will you?"

Hazel stepped up between John and Phoebe and quick as a snake handcuffed them together.

"What the hell is this?" Phoebe demanded holding up their joined wrists.

Hazel cleared her throat. "Every year on this date, we host Blue Moon's Annual Sit-In. And every year we choose a worthy cause that the whole town can agree upon. We host a community fair and donate all proceeds to that cause."

"Hazel, seriously, now is not a good time," John began again.

"Shut up, John," she said amicably and pulled a wadded-up piece of paper from her pocket.

"This year, Blue Moon really stepped up. We raised—"

Bruce broke into a drum roll.

"Thank you, Bruce." Hazel rolled her eyes. "We raised $21,732."

Bruce stopped drumming and bumbled over to Hazel, the cymbals between his knees crashing. He handed something over with a flourish.

Hazel turned to Phoebe, grabbed her uncuffed hand, and slapped a check in it.

Phoebe stared down at it. It was made out to her parents.

"What? What is this?" Shocked, she slid down onto the porch step behind her, her cuffed hand hanging over her head. John tried to slip his arm around her and only succeeded in bending her arm behind her back.

But she couldn't even feel the pain. Not with so much love, so bright and fierce like the sun, glowing inside her.

"We take care of our own," Hazel said briskly.

Phoebe looked up at her. "I'm not one of you."

"Oh, yes you are," Elvira argued. "And it'll be official as soon as you marry this one." She jerked her thumb in John's direction.

The crowd cheered.

"Did you know?" Phoebe whispered to John.

"Of course not. Do you think I'd let you drive away from me *and* twenty thousand dollars?"

She raised an eyebrow. "If short-term memory serves, you were willing to let me drive away from you."

"I was stupid. Insane. An idiot. I must have had a stroke."

She stared hard at the check and its looping numbers. She held in her hand her family's salvation. And Blue Moon had given it to her. No stipulations, no requirements, just pure generosity.

"I don't know how to accept this. It's too much, too big. How can I ever say thank you?" Tears clouded her vision until she saw nothing but a blur of color sweeping out before her. They spilled over, hot on her cheeks.

"You can spend the rest of your life here with the rest of us," Bruce suggested.

"They're not going to start chanting 'Join us, join us,' are they?" Phoebe murmured up at John.

"Wouldn't put it past them." He wrapped his free arm

around her waist and pulled her back to her feet. "But remember, you're mine first and a Mooner second."

"What would you have done if I hadn't come back?"

"Drank every beer in the fridge, polished off your wine, and when I sobered up, I was going to come find you and beg for your forgiveness."

"This way is a lot more efficient."

"How are you going to stand spending your life with such an idiot?" John asked, tracing her jaw tenderly with the tip of his finger.

She sighed at the feelings that swamped her at his touch. "You can make it up to me by giving me all girls."

John sealed the deal with a kiss that Phoebe would remember for the rest of her life.

GROWING

24

*J*ohn didn't give her girls. He gave Phoebe three boys, each the spitting image of him. On the outside, there wasn't a hint of Phoebe on a single one of them. But she'd made her mark on the inside. They were headstrong, stubborn to a fault, and had little regard for consequences.

And most days, Phoebe couldn't imagine her life any other way.

But not today. Today, she was deciding which one of those little monsters she was going to murder first.

Carter, the leader at six, still held the kitchen shears proudly in his little hands. He stood next to his younger brother Beckett. At four, Beckett was the middle child, and despite what so much psychology touted, the kid would never be overlooked. At least, not with the haircut his big brother had just given him.

There were bald spots. Bald spots for God's sake on his little head. And he was strutting around as if he'd just dropped eight bucks at the Snip Shack for a professional job.

Phoebe rubbed a hand over her face, her wedding band

cool on her overheated forehead. Usually she looked at the slim gold band and sent up a prayer of gratitude for her husband. Tonight, however, she cursed his name. John Pierce had done this to her.

She had a master's degree for God's sake. That was no preparation for dealing with these hellions.

"Okay, boys," she breathed, trying to lull them into confessing with a calm tone. "Carter, why did you think Beckett needed you to cut his hair."

"Well, Mom." It was always 'mom' from Carter, never 'mama' or 'mommy.' Beneath his six-year-old surface, the kid was forty years old. "You said you had to give us all haircuts 'cuz of pictures, and you know Beckett gets scared of the clippers. So I used scissors." He was so proud of his problem-solving.

Oh, my God. The family pictures John had scheduled for them at Sears.

"You like it, Mama?" Beckett grinned, showing two missing teeth. One had been a legitimate loose tooth. The other a casualty of little brother Jax shoving him off the merry-go-round at the park.

Speak of the devil, bare feet hustled down the hallway. "Mama, I no feel good—" Jax, two, with only a diaper and t-shirt stepped into the kitchen.

"Honey, where are your pants?" The damn kid was constantly stripping.

He didn't answer. At least, not with words. With the natural forces of a volcano, Jax spewed vomit in a perfect 180-degree arc.

"Oh, sweet Jesus." For one shining moment, Phoebe felt a deep and abiding sense of gratitude that they'd decided to get one more year out of the hideous orange linoleum floor.

Forgetting about the older two non-puking sons, Phoebe

grabbed Jax under the arms and put him in the sink. He went yellow again, and she had just enough time to hand him a soup pot to throw up into. The phone was ringing, and Phoebe gathered every dish towel from the drawer and sprinted for the puke pond. She tossed the towels down and snatched the phone off the wall.

"Hello?" she shouted into it.

"Is now a bad time?" her dearest friend Elvira asked. Phoebe could hear the smile in her voice.

"Why did you let me get married and have three boys? Why didn't you tell me to buy a nice little cottage in the woods and not drive myself insane?"

"What's that beeping?" Elvira asked.

Phoebe muttered a string of curses. "Just the smoke detector. I apparently just charcoaled dinner." Her beautiful casserole, one of John's favorites, was pumping black smoke through the oven vents.

She pushed the towels through Jax's puddle and went running for the stove when it registered. "Oh, my God, Jax, why is your vomit blue?"

"Mama," Jax wailed, hot tears streaming down his chubby little cheeks.

"What did you eat?" Jesus, did he find drain cleaner somewhere? "El, what color is drain cleaner?"

"Green, or yellowish green I think." Phoebe breathed a sigh of relief and switched off the oven knob. "But laundry detergent's blue."

"Jackson Scott, did you eat laundry detergent?" Her voice was so high Murdock, covered snout to stump in mud, came charging into the kitchen from the side door. His fur was ruffled, ready to fight off whatever invader made his mommy scream like that.

194

"Mom, I saw him eating booberry pie upstairs," Carter announced helpfully.

"Blueberry, honey," Phoebe corrected him automatically.

"That's what I said. *Boo*berry."

"Where did he get—" Phoebe turned in his direction and shrieked. "Beckett! Stop cutting your brother's hair this instant!"

Beckett did a little dance and pointed at his brother. "Look, mama. We match!" Carter was indeed now sporting his own bald spot and lopsided bangs.

"Oh, shit."

Carter's little mouth formed a perfect 'o'. "Mom, that's a bad word!"

"Murdock, NO!" Phoebe's scream was loud enough to be heard halfway into town, but it had no effect on the dog that made a beeline for the pile of barf and towels. "JOHN!"

Her husband, her hero, the man who loved her even when she was shrieking like a banshee, sprinted into the kitchen from the side door. The sloppy yellow lab hot on his heels. His entrance scared Murdock who skittered through the outskirts of the puddle, leaving puke paw prints in his dash, to the relative safety of the kitchen table. Phoebe didn't realize she was still holding the phone, its cord stretched across the room. John didn't see it either, and it caught him like a trip wire across the shins.

All six-feet two-inches of him went down in a heap. "Mother of God, what am I laying in?"

"What the hell is happening over there? Do I need to call Hazel?" Elvira demanded.

"I gotta go, El. John just fell in blueberry puke."

∿

Ten minutes later, John stripped to his underwear was giving Jax and Murdock a bath in the sink while Phoebe worked the vomit and child hair and mud into a manageable pile. Carter and Beckett were sitting at the kitchen table eating cold cereal for their dinner. The casserole had finally stopped smoking on the counter.

"We're going to need a new broom," she said, eyeing the bristles of the one she held with the emptiness of a survivor going into shock.

"Do you remember your first summer here?" John asked as he used a dish towel on Jax's head.

Phoebe closed her eyes and remembered it wistfully. "Just you and me. All those long nights and quiet mornings."

"No one wanting to watch Mr. Rogers," John continued.

"Mr. Rogers on, daddy?" Jax asked hopefully.

"No, buddy. Not tonight." His words were gentle, loving, even though Phoebe knew he was as close to the breaking point as she was.

At least she'd been dead right with that choice. Her husband, the love of her ridiculous life, was a constant source of joy and support and commiseration.

"Maybe we should take Rose up on her offer to take the b-o-y-s for a week?" Phoebe suggested hopefully.

John shot her a look. "What has your sister ever done to us that would deserve that?"

"I'm desperate. I don't know what I'm saying. I'm one tiny infraction away from burning this house down and walking away, talking to the voices in my head."

The doorbell sounded, and before Phoebe could decide to just hide under the table and wish it all away, Beckett charged down the hallway to the front door.

"Hi ya, Evywa!"

"Hey, cutie. Is your Mom still alive?"

"She wooks stressed," he said as if a four-year-old knew what stress was. "Is dat pizza?"

On the word "pizza" Carter hurdled the puddle of nasty and joined his brother at the door.

"Oh, hi, Mrs. Normedann,"

Oh, hell. Phoebe was not prepared to deal with Mrs. Nordemann.

"Nordemann, sweetie," Mrs. Nordemann corrected him.

"That's what I said!"

They trooped back down the hall, each footstep sounding to Phoebe like the arrival of a firing squad. Elvira poked her head into the room and shook her head. "Bet you're never going to question my life choices again," she teased Phoebe.

Phoebe burst into tears.

Mrs. Nordemann hopped neatly over the vomit and mud and towels and patted Phoebe on the back. "There, there, my dear. Everything is going to be just fine. This is nothing we can't handle."

"We?" Phoebe wailed.

"We're all family. No one can do this," she gave the chaos a sweeping glance, "alone."

"First thing's first. Boys, pizza. Oh, dear lord, what happened to your hair?" Mrs. Nordemann clapped a hand over her mouth.

"We cutted it!" Beckett announced.

"With scissors," Carter added, eyeing up the pizza boxes.

"Well, we can't do anything about that right now," Elvira sighed. "Go, upstairs and wash your hands and bring a diaper and pants down for your brother."

Phoebe watched in teary disbelief as her boys scrambled to obey.

"What magic power do you have?"

"It's called Peace of Pizza," Elvira said, wiggling the box. "In my experience, men do anything for food."

"Peesa, daddy! Peesa!" Jax squealed.

"Jesus, kid, didn't you just puke up a week's worth of pie?" John asked, plucking his son out of the sink.

"I've got him," Mrs. Nordemann announced, plucking the wet and wiggly toddler out of John's hands and wrapping him in the only clean dish towel left in the house.

"Watch out," John warned. "Sometimes he pees after a bath."

"I peed in da sink," Jax said, stretching his arms out for the pizza across the kitchen.

"Add disinfect sink to the list," Mrs. Nordemann called out to Elvira.

The doorbell rang again, and Carter and Beckett opened it on their way downstairs.

"Hi, Unca Mike! Come in!" Beckett said grandly.

"There's pizza," Carter told him.

The boys, followed by Michael Cardona who was holding his son and an overnight bag, returned to the kitchen.

"Mom, here's the pie plate. Found it in Jax's room," Carter announced, flinging the empty dish at her.

"Jackson, you ate an entire pie? That was for the bake sale tomorrow."

"Elvira, add pie to the list," Mrs. Nordemann said, expertly diapering Jax.

"What list?" John asked, coming up behind Phoebe and wrapping his arms around her as if they were a rock in the midst of a storm.

Michael plopped his son down at the table. "Stay there and have some pizza, Donovan," he told the little blond boy.

"'kay, daddy!"

Beckett leaned in and put his arm around his friend.

"Can someone tell us what's happening?" Phoebe asked weakly.

Elvira shoveled the mass of mess away from the door and straightened. She handed Phoebe a set of keys.

"You two are packing a bag and spending the night at my house. There is a bottle of pinot on the counter and a six-pack of Budweiser in the fridge. If any 'activity' happens in my bed, you will wash the sheets before you leave."

Mrs. Nordemann deposited a freshly diapered and dressed Jax at the table where he promptly stole Carter's slice of pizza.

"Hey! That's mine! M-O-M!"

"Do not respond to that," Elvira said, shoving Phoebe and John toward the stairs. "Pretend they do not exist. Jillian and I are cleaning and baking. Michael and I are spending the night. Hazel's on call, but she'll be here in the morning."

"We can't ask you to do that—" John's argument was interrupted by Elvira's shake of her curls.

"This is what we do. Parenthood is a festering nightmare dotted with moments of truly blissful wonderment. This is not one of those moments. This is a time when we can step in and give you a bit of breathing room so you can come back tomorrow with some sanity."

Phoebe opened her mouth to say thank you, to argue, to tell Elvira she was the most wonderful person in the world. But all that came were more tears.

"Before you feel like a charity case, we do this for everyone. There has never been a couple with kids in Blue Moon who hasn't needed and deserved a break."

"Get the hell out of here," Michael called from the kitchen doorway. "We've got this covered."

"Are we havin' a sleep over?" Carter's voice piped up from the kitchen.

"Sure are, bud," Michael told him.

A chorus of "yays" echoed through the kitchen.

"Cardona," John began.

"You guys took Donovan overnight last month when we were four seconds away from locking him out of the house and pretending we moved," Michael said, cutting off any argument.

"Donovan is one extra kid to us," Phoebe told him. "This is three extras. With access to blueberry pie and scissors. And sometimes Jax wakes up in the middle of the night—"

"We've got this," Elvira said, nudging her toward the stairs. "Go pack a change of clothes, and I don't want to see your face before ten tomorrow morning."

"The dogs need fed. The cats, too. The cows and horses are done, I think. John did you feed the donkey—" Phoebe ran through her mental list.

Elvira pinched Phoebe's lips shut. "We've got this. No one is going to starve to death or be neglected by 10 a.m. tomorrow."

Phoebe's brain did the math. Sixteen hours of uninterrupted peace. Sixteen hours of not hearing "Mom, Mama, Mom." Sixteen hours of peeing by herself. *My God, she could take a shower!* She looked at John and saw the spark of hope in his beautiful gray eyes. Sixteen hours of enjoying each other.

"Yeah, I see that look. Wash my sheets," Elvira reminded them.

25

*a*t 9:59 the next morning a brand-new Phoebe returned home. John, loose and relaxed behind the wheel next to her, sighed.

"I was planning on working another hour on the transmission last night after dinner." His fingers toyed with the skin on the back of her neck.

"And leave me alone with those three monsters again?" she teased.

"I didn't say it was a *good* plan. But I thought if I got the transmission working last night, I could get a jump on spraying this morning. Then we could take the rest of the day off. Swim in the pond or go into town for ice cream. Wear the boys out so I could enjoy some more quiet, quality time with my wife after they fell asleep."

His hand brushed her hair back from her face. She'd cut it shorter a year ago. It came to her shoulders now, straight as an arrow. It was easier than taking care of her long tresses that were irresistible to little fingers that gripped and pulled. But there was still enough of it for John to run his fingers through.

"With a locked door this time," Phoebe reminded him.

"We don't need Jax asking even more questions about naked wrestling."

The corner of John's mouth turned up. "I swear I locked it last time. I don't know how those buggers got in there."

Seven years in, and he was still the sexiest man on the planet to her. He still felt like home and heaven and everything good and steady in her life. The life they'd built together —sure, it was a mess sometimes—but it was a damn good mess.

Phoebe rested her hand on his thigh and squeezed. "I love you, John Pierce, grower of sunflowers and raiser of boys."

Tenderly, he pulled her across the bench seat of his truck to him. "And I love you, Phoebe Allen Pierce. Keeper of books and tender of children and pets."

He kissed her softly, sweetly. A gentle reminder that even when all else was chaos, this, *this* was good and safe and solid and oh so right.

She cupped his face, enjoying the scratch of stubble on her palm. "Maybe if I pack you a sandwich, you can work through lunch, and we can still take the boys into town for ice cream tonight?"

"Sounds like a plan, my brilliant wife."

They got out of the truck and took a moment to stare up at the house.

"You know," Phoebe sighed. "I'm awfully glad I was your Mrs. Pierce. It would have been a shame for you to have to tear this place down and build from scratch."

He laughed. "I'm awfully glad you came back and yelled some sense into me that day." He brushed his lips over her cheek. "Are you ready?"

She bit her lip. "As insane as they drive me, I missed them last night," she confessed.

"That's the Pierce charm," he said with a wink.

Their boys burst through the front door still in their pajamas. "Mom! Daddy! Mama!" Little voices greeted them, little arms embraced them, and in motherly amnesia, Phoebe forgot all about the disaster of last night and let herself love.

"We played Atari with Uncle Mike!"

"Me ate fwee eggs!"

"Can Donovan wiv wiff us?"

Michael, Hazel, and Elvira joined the party on the porch with coffee mugs and donuts.

Phoebe settled Beckett on her hip while John hefted Jackson over his shoulder. Carter hopped on his father's back.

"Thank you just doesn't seem like enough." Phoebe leaned in to wrap Elvira in a well-earned, one-armed hug.

Elvira smirked. "Please. Piece of cake. I don't know what you parents are always complaining about," she winked.

John, juggling Jax, exchanged a shoulder slapping manshake with Michael.

"Welcome home," Hazel said, pressing a coffee cup into Phoebe's hand.

"I'm afraid to go inside," Phoebe whispered.

Hazel's laugh boomed under the porch roof. "There's no puke. I promise."

"I frowed up yesterday," Jax announced cheerfully from John's arms.

"He gets his emotional eating from me," Phoebe joked.

Donovan wrapped his chubby little arms around her leg. "My Mommy and Daddy wrestle nakeds just like you and Uncca John!"

"Oh, lord." Phoebe clamped a hand over Donovan's mouth.

"Let's see if we can dig up some booze for that coffee," Hazel said, red-faced.

"Kitchen pantry behind the wheat bran," Phoebe called after her.

With her arms full of boys, she stepped into the house that no longer smelled like blueberry vomit. It smelled lemony with a hint of lavender. The living room had been redecorated with a large quilt and cushion fort bursting with blankets and pillows. The hallway floor was swept clean, and there wasn't a speck of dust on any of the picture frames dotting the entryway walls.

Gone was the puddle of disgustingness. The linoleum gleamed brighter than new. The kitchen counters were clear, the breakfast dishes were drying next to the sink, and there was a full pot of coffee on.

"I know John is my husband and all, but I'd marry each and every one of you for this," Phoebe said, feeling her eyes grow misty.

Murdock, the aging canine who refused to embrace his elderliness, woke in his bed in the corner. His rear end wagged, and he let out a greeting yip before rolling onto his back and falling asleep again. Sadie, the dopic retriever John had found on the roadside with a broken leg, danced at their feet until one of the cats wandered through the kitchen drawing her attention.

"Let's see," Elvira said. "Nordemann worked her magic on your casserole dish. I don't know how she got that charcoal brick out of it, but it's good as new. The dishtowels were a complete loss. Hazel picked some new ones up on her way in this morning. The boys had breakfast. Laundry's done and hanging out on the line. And there's sandwich fixings for lunch."

"Alfie Cofax and Carson showed up at six a.m. and should be finished with the spraying by noon," Hazel put in. John swiped a hand over his face and rubbed the back of his neck.

"There's also a new deadbolt on your bedroom door after MacGyver here announced that he learned to pick your lock," Michael said, jerking his thumb in Carter's direction.

"Carter!" Phoebe gasped impressed and horrified.

He shrugged his shoulders, a move that was one hundred percent Phoebe. "Beckett locked me out once, an' I didn't like it."

John, in a rare display of emotion, grabbed Elvira by the shoulders and placed a loud kiss on her mouth. The boys cackled when he repeated the same with Hazel and even Michael.

"Who wants one more game of *Super Mario*?" Michael asked, clapping his hands. He winked at his wife.

Hands shot up around the room, including John's.

"Go play with your friends, Michael," Hazel grinned.

Team Testosterone stampeded into the living room, and Phoebe sat down at the table. "I honestly don't know what I'd do without all of you."

"You'll never have to find out," Elvira promised, squeezing her hand and sliding the donuts closer.

"What's this?" Phoebe asked, fingering the envelope on the table.

"It's an application from Nordemann. She's starting up some committee for the betterment of Blue Moon," Hazel rolled her eyes.

"Calls it the Beautification Committee," Elvira put in.

"Just what I need. One more responsibility," Phoebe groaned. But in Blue Moon, civic duty was the law of the land. And there was no way she'd say no to the woman who cleaned up partially digested pie on her kitchen floor.

"It's probably going to end up like Tupperware parties. Lots of gossip and wine and appetizers," Elvira said. "I'm joining."

"Well, that doesn't sound too bad. And I could use a little time away from my army of adorable assholes. I mean, I love them more than anything in this universe, but sometimes I just want to drive away and never come back."

Hazel laughed. "I know exactly how you feel. Sign me up for this Beautification thing."

Elvira topped off everyone's mugs.

"Phoebs, you're doing a great job. Your boys are wonderful people. Wonderful people with terrible haircuts, but still. You and John are doing it right." Hazel said, sipping her coffee. She wasn't one to wear her feelings on her sleeve, which made the words even more powerful.

"Be proud. They're going to grow into fine men," Elvira predicted.

26

One of Phoebe's "fine men" was strutting around her kitchen like a peacock on a summer afternoon. Beckett had *the look*.

Her little boy was sixteen years old and enjoying his junior year of high school. She should have seen it coming. Especially when he asked to borrow her SUV last night.

Damn that Moon Beam Parker and her teenage breasts, Phoebe cursed.

Great. Now she had to add "sanitize the backseat" to her lengthy to do list in between bookkeeping clients.

Beckett picked up the coffee pot whistling cheerfully.

"What are you doing?" Phoebe demanded.

He shrugged. "Felt like coffee this morning."

"You don't drink coffee. You drink hot cocoa and soda and Gatorade."

That Pierce smirk played upon his lips. Oh, hell. Was that a *hickey* on his neck?

"Does Dad need help today? I can give him a few hours before Carter takes me into town. I'm taking Moon Beam to the movies."

She nodded, trying not to choke when he mentioned Moon Beam's name. "That would be great."

"Did you talk to Dad about your proposal?" Beckett asked, reaching for the pitcher of cream.

"Not yet. I want to go over it one more time."

"Mom," he laid a hand on her shoulder. "Sometimes you just have to pull the trigger. A farmer's market in the park is a great idea, and the sooner you bring it up to Dad, the sooner we can get Mayor Nordemann to bring it up at a town meeting."

Phoebe's heart ached. Beckett was such a good, solid boy. He was as invested in Pierce Acres and Blue Moon as John was and for all the right reasons. He loved fiercely and dreamed big. And now her little boy was having sex. God, she wasn't ready to go through this again. Carter at least had hidden it better. It had taken Phoebe nearly a week to pry the truth out of him.

Jackson, her baby, strolled through the door. At fourteen, he was still more boy than man. He was outgoing like she was but had an artistic side that reminded her so much of John. She'd caught him writing in notebooks this past summer. And just like his father, he'd refused to let her read anything he'd written.

At the moment, Phoebe wanted to hug him until he promised to never outgrow her.

"Morning, Ma," he said, giving her a peck on her cheek and rummaging for fruity-o's. Yes, she'd hang on to Jax as long as he'd let her and save him from the Moon Beam Parkers of the world.

John, dressed for a day in the fields, waltzed in next. "Morning, my brilliant wife." He said, pressing a very non-platonic kiss on her mouth. Beckett hadn't been the only Pierce enjoying the expression of biological urges last night.

Phoebe pointed at Beckett, her frown fierce.

John peered over her shoulder. *What?* he mouthed.

Phoebe circled her face with her finger and pointed at Beckett again.

John frowned, still missing it.

Phoebe tapped her own neck and again pointed in Beckett's direction.

Beckett turned pouring a waterfall of sugar into his mug. "Morning, Pops."

"Christ. Not him, too," John sighed. "I feel like we just went through this with Carter."

"Go talk to him," she whispered through clenched teeth. She looked at Jax, shoveling in the fruity-o's while reading the Sunday comics. "Both of them."

It was a benefit of having boys, she supposed. John handled the bulk of the potty-training, teaching the boys the joy of pissing in nature or off the porch. And now he was stuck with the sex ed, too.

"What do you want me to say?" Her dear husband looked both proud and panicked.

"Condoms, respect, no means hell fucking no," she ticked the items off on her fingers as she hissed at him.

"You sound more prepared. Maybe you should handle this—"

"Go!" Phoebe growled and softened it with a wink.

Beckett's coffee, now a pale khaki color thanks to the gallon of cream he'd added, sloshed over the rim of his mug as John grabbed him by the back of the neck.

"Outside," John muttered.

"What the hell, dad? I didn't do anything."

"Tell that to the hickey on your neck. You too, Jackson. Porch. Now."

27

*P*hoebe gave them all of ten seconds after the front door slammed behind them before sneaking to the open living room window. She wanted to make sure John hit all the points so she wouldn't have to do a follow-up lecture like the one that had embarrassed the hell out of Carter.

She curled into the worn sofa and pressed her face against the back cushion, listening.

"So, you and Moon Beam Parker," John began.

"H-how did you know?" Beckett stuttered.

Phoebe smiled. Her boys thought she and John were psychic half the time. The lovable idiots just didn't realize how transparent they were. Thank God she hadn't raised sneaky teenage girls like she had been. She'd raised boys who were so bad at lying she knew it was false before the words tumbled out of their mouths.

"Jesus, Beckett. You're strutting around like a prize-winning hog. An idiot could tell you had sex last night."

"You had sex with Moon Beam Parker?" Jax asked, awed.

Phoebe heard the resounding slap of a high-five and gritted her teeth together. Men were idiots, she decided.

"Don't be an asshole," John said. Phoebe heard a different smack and knew John had just cuffed Beckett on the back of the head.

"Ouch! Geez, Dad!"

John sighed. "Let's start with the basics, and then we'll work our way up to why a high-five over sex makes you an asshole. Did you use a condom?"

"Of course, Dad. And she's on the pill, too."

Phoebe peered through the screen and saw John holding up a hand. Her poor husband. Even though he was a life-long Blue Mooner, he still operated under the misconstrued assumption that people deserved their privacy. "Are you two dating?" he asked.

Beckett nodded, his expression dreamy. "I think I love her, Dad."

Jax made barfing sounds. Given his track record of binging on sugary snacks until his body rejected everything, Phoebe looked to make sure he was just joking and not spewing fruity-o's on the porch she'd swept off just that morning.

Beckett in love with Moon Beam? If that was love, then Phoebe would shave her head and change her name to Mrs. Clean. He didn't know what love was yet. And she bet money that Moon Beam would not be Mrs. Beckett Pierce in however many years it took her son to finish that law degree he was already talking about.

John cleared his throat. "Well, son, I'm glad to hear that you have strong feelings for her," he said diplomatically. "Sex is this great thing—"

"You don't have to tell me," Beckett grinned, happy to finally be part of the club.

Phoebe rolled her eyes heavenward.

"Shut up," John sighed. "Sex between two people who care

about each other is the best sex there is. Don't waste your time when you don't have feelings because it'll never compare."

Phoebe nodded, approving his point.

"So, it's better with someone you like?" Jax asked, frowning.

"Okay, it's like this," John said, swiping a hand over his mouth.

Phoebe felt a sliver of guilt. She should have at least let him have some coffee before pushing him into *The Talk*.

"You know how peanut butter brownie explosion is your favorite ice cream?"

Jax nodded enthusiastically, his expression now close to Beckett's post-virginity-loss awe. "Oh, yeah."

"Well, imagine instead of going for peanut butter brownie explosion you go for mint chocolate chip."

"Why would I do that?" Jax asked, clearly confounded.

"Well, that's my point. When you know what's best, don't waste your time fooling around with women or ice cream that you don't really like."

"Very sage, Dad," Beckett snorted.

"So, you did two things right," John said, shifting the conversation back to Beckett. "You used protection, and you care about the girl."

Beckett preened.

"But that's like saying, you're ready to drive a car just because you know which pedal's the brake and which is the gas. There's a lot more to it. Consent."

Beckett's face lost every ounce of color. "Jesus, Dad! You don't think I'd—"

"Relax, son. No, I don't think you'd ever do that. You're a good man. But it still deserves discussing."

"Do what?" Jax demanded, confused.

Beckett turned to his brother. "Never, ever, ever, coerce a

woman into sex. Or I will show up on your doorstep and kick your ass before murdering you."

John nodded approvingly.

"Jeez!" Jax winced. "Why would anyone do that? Coerce, I mean."

"Some people are assholes," Beckett said. "That's what Carter told me, Dad. The condoms were from his stash, but he made me promise to be respectful—as if I wouldn't be," Beckett scoffed.

Phoebe hugged a pillow into her chest. Carter, eighteen and preparing for the Army after graduation, had absorbed enough of those lessons to pass them on to his brother. They were doing something right.

"Now, Beckett. I know you, and I know your brothers. I know none of you would ever force a woman to do anything she's not one hundred percent excited about."

Jackson snickered. "Sorry. I was just picturing you trying to coerce Mom into anything."

Phoebe grinned to herself.

"That's exactly the kind of woman... or man—no judg-ment—that I hope you each end up with. Your mother is a strong, smart, incredible woman who is brave enough to stand up for herself and others. What I worry about for you boys is running across someone who isn't as, shall we say 'vocal,' in her opinions or firm with their boundaries."

"What are you trying to say, Dad?" Jax asked.

Beckett was frowning too.

"Jesus, I wish I had some coffee in me," John muttered to himself. "Alright. Let's go back to the ice cream. Beckett, say you call up Moon Beam and ask her to go for ice cream."

"Sure. Okay. Can I borrow Mom's car?"

"Focus, son. So, you call her up, she says yes to ice cream. But then she calls you back and says she's changed her mind."

"Why would she do that?" Jax asked, devastated at the possibility.

John gave a short laugh. "I can't believe this is how I'm spending my Saturday morning. No one knows why she changed her mind, and the point is it doesn't matter why. It means her answer is now no. So, should Beckett show up to her house and drag her into the car and force her to go for ice cream?"

"No, but I think he should swing her by the doctor's if she's saying no to ice cream."

Beckett punched his brother in the shoulder. "Ice cream is *sex*, man. Keep up."

"Oh. No wonder I like it so much," Jax grinned.

"If I get through this without decking you both, it'll be a miracle," John sighed. His sons grinned at him, unaffected by the threat.

"Okay. Back to the ice cream sex," Jax said. "If Moon Beam says no to ice cream sex, then it would be dickish if Beckett tried to force her to go for ice cream sex."

"Exactly," John nodded. "Dickish *and* illegal. Even if she said yes first, that doesn't matter, and if I ever hear of one of you throwing that excuse in someone's face, I'll kick your ass before I murder you."

"Got it," Beckett saluted

"Okay, now let's fast forward a few years. Say you're with a girl at a party, and she says yes. You go someplace private, and she falls asleep or she's had too much to drink and passes out. What do you do?"

"Well, you sure as hell don't give her ice cream. She could choke on it and die or something," Jax reasoned.

"Sex, dummy. He's still talking about sex."

"I *know* that. It's the same thing. Why would you feed a

passed-out girl ice cream is the same as why would you try to have sex with her."

"Good boy," John nodded. "To recap, she needs to feel safe enough to say yes, to be physically capable of saying yes, and if she changes her mind for any reason, you respect that or the ass-kicking and murdering happen.

Beckett saluted. "Got it, Dad. We won't let you down."

"I know you two won't. You boys are turning out to be a lot smarter and more thoughtful than I was at your age. Now, do we need to talk about the mechanics of how to make sure you're doing it well?"

Beckett's grin split his face. "No, sir. I think I got that part down. There were no complaints last night. Carter says, 'Your focus should always be on the girl and making her feel good.'" His spot-on impression of his older brother made Phoebe smile.

"And that's why high-fiving over sex is immature. A woman isn't a touchdown or a solid burn on your buddy. If anything, you should fall down and kiss her feet in gratitude," John said.

"Is that what you do to Mom?" Jax asked like the true smart ass he was.

"You're damn right I do," John told him without a hint of shame. "Right before I start apologizing for giving her three thick-headed boys."

Jax grinned.

"Sex is just like everything else worthwhile in this world. It's about having a healthy respect. It's a big deal, and it sounds like you did everything right, Beckett. So, congratulations, son." He held out his hand to Beckett who shook it and beamed like a lighthouse beacon.

"Thanks, Dad."

"Make sure you keep making the right choices. And Jax,

when the time comes for you, I want you to remember all this."

"Ice cream," Jax nodded.

Phoebe peeked through the window and saw the Jeep wheel into the driveway. The stereo was blaring '80s rock, and Carter, their oldest, hopped out looking handsome and entirely too grown up. He hauled his camping gear out of the back and climbed the porch. One look at Beckett's face had him grinning.

"Well, well, well, little brother's not so little anymore," he said.

"How can you tell? Do you think everyone at school will be able to tell?" Beckett demanded.

"If you keep prancing around with that shit-eating grin on your face, I think even the lunch ladies will know," Carter said, slipping his sunglasses into the neck of his t-shirt.

"Dad just gave us the talk," Jax announced.

Carter ruffled his youngest brother's hair. "Did he go with ice cream?" he asked, and they all laughed.

Phoebe's heart was full. They were raising good men. And how could they not turn out that way? With John Pierce as their living, breathing example. The man was a miracle to her each and every day and so were her boys.

"Now, let's talk about vehicles," John began. "Beckett, you're going to detail the interior and anywhere else naked body parts touched before your mom drives her car anywhere, and then we're going to break into your savings and go find you something to drive."

Beckett whooped. "This is seriously like the best day of my life. Wanna come, guys?"

Carter grinned. "Wouldn't miss it. Ernest Washington's got some pretty nice rides on his lot."

"Think he'd open up early for us?" Beckett asked John.

"He's probably already heard your news and is picking out all the cars with big backseats," John teased.

"You coming with us, Jax?" Beckett asked.

Jax was already nodding when five-and-a-half feet of leggy teenage brunette strolled up the drive wheeling her bike. "Morning," she said, tossing her hair over her shoulder. "Thought I'd come out and visit the horses if you don't mind."

Phoebe smiled. Joey Greer was the closest thing she had to a daughter. She was in Jackson's grade, and the two had been thick as thieves since kindergarten. She wouldn't be surprised if someday Joey became her daughter-in-law.

John waved the girl up on the porch. "You're always welcome here, Joey. And there's ten bucks in it for you if you take Rusty out for a ride. He didn't get out yesterday."

"You don't need to pay me," she said dreamily. "I should be paying you."

"Don't be silly. We've got horses. You love horses. It's the perfect arrangement."

"Still, I'd feel better if you didn't try to pay me all the time," Joey said, all serious brown eyes.

"I'll do my best not to pay you if you promise to be careful."

"Ride with a helmet and always in view of the barn or house," she recited.

"Good girl."

"We're going car shopping, Joey," Beckett announced. "You want to come along?" She was as much a sister to Beckett as daughter to Phoebe and John.

Phoebe watched as Joey blushed, shaking her head. "Nah. Thanks though. I think I'll take the horses out."

"I think I'll stay, too," Jax said. "Maybe I'll ride with you."

Joey looked up at him like he'd just told her he was an

astronaut who cured cancer. Grinning, Phoebe slid off the couch and snuck back into the kitchen.

When she pushed through the screen door, steaming cup of coffee in hand, John's eyes lit up. The boys were busy trying to decide what kind of car Beckett should get. Joey was staring longingly at the barn. Sadie chased Tripod the three-legged cat under the fence into Leopold the donkey's pasture.

"Thank you," John whispered, accepting the mug.

She shook her head. "Uh-uh. Thank *you*."

There just weren't enough thank yous in this world. She had everything her heart ever could have wanted right here on this land.

She leaned in and kissed John long and hard until the boys all made vomiting noises.

HARVEST

28

*P*hoebe rested her forehead against the glass of the car window and hoped that the coolness would quell the throbbing in her head. Carter, her quiet, steadfast rock, was behind the wheel. Beckett, the perpetual leader, and Jax, the creative troublemaker, rode silently in the backseat as they drove away from the hospital, away from John.

His death had been peaceful, beautiful almost. He'd passed with his sons surrounding his bed, his hand clasped in hers, and the faintest hint of a smile on his lips. With a quiet whisper of "thank you," John Pierce was gone from her life forever.

From diagnosis to death, it had been a handful of months. Not nearly enough time to prepare.

She felt... Phoebe wasn't sure how she felt. His suffering was over. Never again would he face another treatment more painful and withering than the disease it fought. Never again would he try to hide the bone-deep pain from those who hurt for him. He was finally free, and she was going home.

Home. The word rang flat in her head. Home was where John was. In the fields, on the tractor, in the bed they'd shared for twenty-six years. Where was home now? Where was her heart now?

Jax, eyes red-rimmed, leaned forward between the seats. "Maybe we should stop and get ice cream?"

The corner of her mouth tugged up. Jax took after her in the emotional eating department, and it looked as though three years in L.A. hadn't changed that about him.

"Ice cream?" Beckett rumbled from the back, his voice raw. "You think ice cream is going to make you feel better right now?"

"It's worth a shot," Jax argued.

Beckett punched Jax in the shoulder. Jax retaliated with a blow to his brother's thigh.

"Ouch!"

"If you two assholes don't knock it off right now, I'm going to dump you on the side of the road, and then Mom and I are going for ice cream," Carter said calmly. He held his hurt further under the surface, Phoebe had noted. Even with everything else happening around them, she'd seen the shadows in her son's eyes. His hurried arrival at the hospital yesterday came on the tail end of twenty-three hours of frantic travel from his assignment in Afghanistan.

Sorries were grumbled from the backseat.

Well, at least that part of her life was intact, familiar. Her sons loved and fought with the same ferociousness. Arguments and tussles should have been left behind them, each one an adult now. But old habits—or family traditions—died hard. And Phoebe tried to take temporary comfort in the familiarity of it.

The bickering picked back up five miles from home. Law student Beckett was trying to discuss the next steps: funeral home, estate lawyer, obituary. Jax weighed in with his opinion that now wasn't the time to start berating their mother with details. Carter mentioned that maybe they both should get their heads out of their asses.

It's important to know what you want. She heard John's voice, clear as day in her head. She let out the breath she didn't know she'd been holding. He was with her. She could feel his calming presence and wished their boys would shut the hell up and feel it to.

It's important to know what you want. He'd told her that their first summer together when she'd been convinced that she had life all figured out. What she would have missed out on had she stayed the course.

If John wanted her to do what she wanted then she'd... well, right this second she wanted some quiet time. Silence. She wanted to lay down on that big bed, on the sheets that still smelled like her husband, her best friend, her partner in life. And she wanted to weep until she had nothing left inside her. And then she wanted to sleep until she could stand the thought of waking up to a world without John.

By the time they pulled into the farm's drive, Phoebe's headache had dug in like a pickaxe behind her eye, and everyone else was yelling. She just needed to get inside, lock the boys out, and let them fight it out in the yard like the old days.

She wanted peace.

But there was a car in the driveway. And her dearest friend Elvira Eustace was sitting on the porch swing holding a casserole dish in her lap. A bottle of wine sat on the cushion next to her.

Phoebe slipped out of the car, leaving her bickering boys behind, and trudged toward the house. Elvira met her at the foot of the porch steps. With the knowing that came from a long friendship, Elvira simply wrapped her arms around Phoebe's shoulders and held her tight.

"He's gone," Phoebe said the words out loud and felt her world crumble just a little more.

"Beckett called," Elvira said.

"It was beautiful and peaceful, and now he's gone, and I don't have an anchor."

"Yes, you do." Elvira's arms tightened around her. "Yes, you do."

Phoebe clung to her friend like a rock in the storm and let loose the tears she'd tamped down. "What am I going to do, El?"

"Whatever the fuck you want, honey."

Phoebe hiccupped out a laugh. "You sound just like him."

"Honey, John Pierce has been spreading his wisdom for years. We *all* sound like him."

Phoebe heard what Elvira wasn't saying. She wasn't the only one who'd lost something wonderful today. They'd all lost him. A father, a friend, a mentor, a neighbor.

"What's in the casserole dish?" Phoebe sniffled.

"Chicken and dumplings."

Phoebe pulled back, swiping her sleeve over her eyes. "John's favorite."

"I figured we could either eat it or dump it on the ground in homage to him."

Laughter through tears was good medicine, Phoebe decided.

"Mom?"

Phoebe turned to face Carter. Her sons stood behind her, broken in their own grief yet ready to hold her together.

"We've got more company," Beckett said, tilting his head toward the parade of cars and trucks turning into their lane.

"Holy shit," Jax muttered.

Elvira's eyes widened. "I swear I didn't tell anyone."

Carter looked guilty. "I may have texted Cardona."

Leading the pack was Michael and Hazel Cardona in Michael's pride and joy, a shiny new red pick-up. Their son, Donovan, followed in his ancient Tahoe. Behind him was another dozen cars.

"Oh, my," Phoebe whispered.

"This isn't a damn party," Carter muttered, and Phoebe heard the hurt behind his words. She laid a hand on his arm.

"Carter, they all lost him, too."

He clenched his jaw and nodded, but she saw the tears glassy in his eyes. *His father's eyes,* she thought.

"Let them do this. They need it as much as we do," she whispered.

He swiped an arm over his eyes, the exact way she had. He'd gotten pieces of them both, she supposed.

"Okay. I'll go dig out the tables."

"Take Jax with you so he doesn't start stress eating everything."

Carter pressed a gentle kiss to her temple. "Love you, Mom."

She couldn't say anything for a moment. Her throat was too tight. So, she just hung on. She released him and patted him on the chest. "I love you, Carter. Now, go on. Might as well get the canopies out, too."

She watched as Carter caught Jax in a friendly headlock and dragged his brother in the direction of the barn. Beckett stepped up and put his hands on her shoulders. "Whenever you want them gone, just say the word," he told her.

"I think this is exactly what we need," she promised him.

"I do, too," he agreed. "Thanks for raising us here, Mom. I can't imagine a better home."

Her eyes clouded for the umpteenth time today. "You better start complaining about your brothers before I start crying again."

Hazel climbed out of the truck. She held a shopping bag of hot dog and hamburger buns. Michael slid a case of beer out of the backseat and looped another bag over his fingers. His eyes were red, his jaw set.

Best friends from birth. That's what John and Michael had been. Everyone here had a history that was rooted around everyone else. It was the beauty and the pain of Blue Moon.

Beckett dropped a kiss on the top of her head. "Love you, Mom. I'm gonna help here, and then I'm going to go fix the canopies. Those two idiots are setting them up all wrong." He winked at her and took the load from Michael. Phoebe pulled the man in for a long, hard hug. She felt his shoulders shake once in a shared grief so sharp it cut the air, making it hurt to breathe.

Michael pulled back half a step. His mouth worked open and closed a few times, but nothing came out. Phoebe patted his cheek. "I feel exactly the same way," she promised him. "Now, go get the grill off the porch and fire it up."

Grief called for movement. Anything to keep you going forward one step and a time.

29

There were tears and watery smiles as an entire town gathered to grieve one of their beloved on the land he'd tended.

For Phoebe, the pain and love curled together into something bright and hot that was fighting to escape her chest. She took a minute to herself, walking back down the drive that John had once wondered if they should pave. But she had loved the cheerful clouds of dust that followed them as they came and went.

Every inch of this farm was home to her. And yet it would never be the same. Not without John Pierce striding through the fields with two dogs and at least one kid on his heels. Not without him taking a moment in the middle of a corn field to just stop, breathe, to honor the pulse of nature. Not without him in their bed or in the kitchen peeking at whatever recipe she'd cooked up for dinner that night.

There wasn't one hole where the man had been. There were a thousand.

She stopped and turned, facing the farm. The pretty little farm house had truly become a home, full to bursting at the seams with love and boys' sports equipment. The red barn had been added on to as their menagerie of pets grew. Melanie II had finally gotten a friend. And then another and another. They had four retired dairy cows that enjoyed sunning themselves in grassy pastures. Leopold the donkey occupied the front pasture and tolerated the dogs and cats that snuck beneath his fence.

She'd wanted chickens but now? Now she wasn't sure. Could she stay here? Could she run Pierce Acres herself? Would she even want to? The appeal of this life had been John. Now what was the appeal?

She heard the engine of a station wagon easing off the shoulder of the road behind Bill Fitzsimmons' Gremlin. The driver was a stranger with fear in his eyes.

"Excuse me, I don't mean to interrupt your party." He was a good-looking man, broad of shoulder and clean-shaven. His hair was graying around the temples, and his eyes crinkled when he smiled up at her. "I was hoping you could tell me how to get to Cleary before my three daughters murder me for insisting that a day trip would be more fun without any technology."

Phoebe found a genuine smile for the man trapped with three annoyed redheads.

One of the girls gave an exasperated sigh. "Dad, I *told* you we need our phones. They have GPS!"

"He's doing the best he can, Em. Your bad vibes aren't helping," the girl in the front seat said, fiddling with the fringes on her halter top. She looked like she belonged in Blue Moon.

"People have been crossing continents for centuries without that beeping, obnoxious 'Make a U-turn' technology," the man argued, mimicking a snooty techno tone.

Phoebe laughed, and it felt like a few knots inside her loosened up enough that she could breathe.

"Serves me right for wanting some uninterrupted quality family time," he sighed out the window to Phoebe.

"They grow up fast," Phoebe said, thinking of her own sons. "Force them into these things as long as it's legal," she advised.

His smile was warm, almost familiar.

The youngest daughter crawled over her sister and stuck her head out the rear window. "Maybe we should stick around here for the day?"

Phoebe followed the girl's gaze to where all six-feet-four-inches of handsome Donovan Cardona wandered past with a deli platter balanced on top of a case of beer. Donovan was as much one of her sons as the three bickering men she'd been tempted to lock out of the house today. However, he generally had more sense.

"Do you have a piece of paper?" Phoebe interrupted the brewing argument in the car. "I can write down the directions for you."

The man pawed through the glove box of his ancient station wagon with desperate hope and triumphantly produced a tablet and a stubby golf pencil.

"I can't thank you enough," he whispered fervently. "You're saving my life right now. They were minutes away from tying me to the roof rack and giving up on the whole adventure."

Phoebe smiled as she scrawled the directions and prominent milestones on the paper. "I'm happy to save a life today."

"If you're ever in Hastings, Connecticut, looking for Italian food, I have a restaurant, and you'll eat for free," he promised. "Amore Italian."

Phoebe handed the paper and pencil over. "I'll keep that in mind," she promised.

"It's amazing food," the girl in the front seat announced. "You won't regret it."

"He's crap with directions but magic in the kitchen." The girls poured the praise on, love over a glossy coat of annoyance, and Phoebe smiled. At least for some, life was beautifully, blessedly normal right now.

The man grinned up at her. "Disaster averted. You have my eternal gratitude, my directional angel of rural upstate New York."

She laughed again, surprised that she was still capable. "It was my pleasure, lost stranger. Good luck on your travels."

A van bumped past them down the lane, and Phoebe spotted three of the kids that made up the Wild Nigels, Blue Moon's best—and only—garage band.

"We'll let you get back to your celebration," he said.

It wasn't a celebration. It was how Blue Moon mourned. She wanted to tell him that but wanted more for the man to have his peace with his daughters. Phoebe waved as they eased down the lane toward the road. She watched them pull out of the drive before starting back the lane to survey the chaos that was her yard and house.

People poured out onto the porch into the front yard. Tables had magically appeared under the ancient oak and were laden with miles of food and gallons of alcohol. There was one measly case of water in a sea of beer and wine.

Phoebe pressed her fingers to her lips, swamped with feeling.

It really was a celebration. John Pierce, that beautiful man, had lived a beautiful life. And his friends and neighbors had turned out to mark the occasion and to show their support. She wasn't alone. No one ever really was in Blue Moon.

She was surrounded, smothered in love freely given. She was woven into the fabric of this town as tightly as if she'd been born here. The town that had saved her family and given her the option to stay.

She'd given back in every way she could think of. She'd been a founding member of the Beautification Committee, finding creative ways to improve the quality of life for townspeople, including a little matchmaking here and there. Seven years ago, she and John had started up Blue Moon's farmer's market on a trial run, and it had been going strong ever since, occupying every square inch of One Love Park Sundays from spring to fall. And, as Mrs. Nordemann and Elvira had once done for her, she'd spent countless nights stepping in for other exhausted couples with small children.

It was a joy to be able to give that kind of support when it was most needed. And that's what all these wonderful people were doing in her yard.

Elvira whistled from the front porch, two glasses of wine in her hands. She raised one in Phoebe's direction, and Phoebe decided she couldn't think of anything she wanted more in the moment.

She threaded her way through the growing throng, accepting hugs and condolences as she went. John's middle school biology teacher, who gave him a C in ninth grade, was there as was the librarian who talked Jax into entering the poetry competition last year. Ernest Washington, the man who'd shown every one of her boys how to change the oil in their cars, was perched on a cooler, harmonica in hand.

Everyone was there.

Her boys found her on the porch, and there was something softer than the keen edge of grief in them all, she thought.

An impromptu wake with equal parts tears and laughter was good medicine. Her heart felt impossibly lighter as if she could feel John smiling down on her at the chaos that reigned in the yard.

30

In the dark, Phoebe spotted a lone figure skulking up the steps of the side porch. She'd know that shadow anywhere.

She waited in the shadows of the porch until the figure had put down the parcel just outside the screen door.

"You leave that cake there, and some drunken mourner is going to step in it," Phoebe said mildly, stepping into the moonlight.

"Shit. You scared the hell out of me, Phoebe." Joey Greer didn't look scared. She looked downright miserable. Phoebe held out her arms, and with the briefest of hesitations, Joey stepped into them. Still after all these years and so much heart ache, she counted this girl a daughter.

She'd been woven into the fabric of their family since the first day of kindergarten in Jax's class. And once upon a time, she'd loved Jax with everything that an eighteen-year-old heart was capable of. An accident, a bad choice, and those days were over. Jax had picked up and left in the middle of the night, and Joey hadn't seen him in the three years since.

Phoebe knew coming here tonight knowing that Jax was here had cost the girl.

"What kind of cake is it?" Phoebe whispered into Joey's chestnut hair.

"Pineapple upside down."

Phoebe smiled. "My favorite. You're a good girl, Joey." She pulled back, brushing Joey's hair away from her pretty face. Her brown eyes were rimmed red. The only truly girly thing Joey enjoyed was baking, and like everything else she did in her life, she was damn good at it.

"What the hell's wrong with everyone?" Joey said, trying to pretend everything was normal.

"That lovable idiot Fitz brought the wrong brownies, and half the town is baked out of their minds on my front lawn right now."

Joey surveyed the bodies upright and otherwise. "What about the other half?"

"Everyone brought casseroles and booze. Anyone who isn't shit-faced is just too full to move."

Joey snorted out a pained laugh. "Okay. Well, I just wanted to..." she gestured toward the cake and shoved her hands in the back pocket of her jeans. "And, uh, if you need anything, let me know."

"I do need something, Joey."

"Anything."

"Take this cake and meet me in the barn in two minutes. I'm going to grab two forks and my emergency bottle of whiskey, and we're going to eat until we're sick."

Tears glistened in Joey's eyes. "But you have... company."

"Don't be stupid. You're family, Joey. Barn. Two minutes. And whatever you do. Do not let anyone near that cake. These people are one step away from pulling the roast from the freezer and licking it."

Joey gave a brusque nod and grabbed the cake.

Phoebe snuck in the side door and had to step over Bruce Oakleigh's legs to get to the utensil drawer. He was sitting against the kitchen island singing something that sounded like Ke$ha's "Tik Tok."

She grabbed two forks and, stepping over Bruce again, tiptoed to the pantry. Behind the flour and the box of wheat bran, which was a disguise for all her snacks that she hid from Jax, she produced a bottle of Jameson and headed for the door.

Amethyst Oakleigh met her on the porch. The woman leaned as if she were on the deck of ship going through rough water. Her brown eyes were bigger than dinner plates. "Escuse me, Phlebe. I was wondering if you've scheen my huschband?" She hiccupped and blinked as if surprised. Amethyst had never been a drinker in her younger years, and as a lifelong lightweight found herself snockered once a year, usually at a town function.

"Nearly passed out on the floor in there," Phoebe said, pointing behind her.

"Thanks to yooou," Amethyst nodded and walked into the screen door.

"You have to pull it open and then walk through," Phoebe called over her shoulder.

"Hey, Mom!"

Jax's voice froze her in her tracks. She hid the whiskey and forks behind her back. "Hi, honey. You doing okay?"

Jax kicked at the ground. "Yeah. Just wanted to see if you needed anything."

Phoebe shoved the forks in her pocket and cupped his face. "Can you make sure no one drives home?"

He nodded morosely. "Yeah. Yeah. I can do that."

"Good boy. Thank you," she started to turn for the barn, but he stopped her.

"Mom, I didn't see Joey here. Do you think she knows?"

"Yeah, honey. I think she knows."

"I'd hate for her to think she couldn't be here with..." he spread his arm wide to encompass the chaos. "Everyone because I'm here."

"Sweetie. We're all responsible for our own decisions. Got it?"

He gave a sullen one-shoulder shrug.

And Phoebe gave his cheek a pinch. "You know Joey. Do you think she'd let anyone scare her off of anything?"

Jax gave her the tiniest of smiles. His handsome face softened for a moment and then tensed again. "Are we going to ever be okay again?"

Phoebe wrapped him in a one-armed hug. "I know we are."

"How?"

"Your dad promised me we would."

"I can't believe he's gone," Jax whispered, his voice soft, strained. "I feel like I didn't get to know him as anything but Dad."

"Oh, baby." Phoebe's heart ached for her son. She'd known John inside and out, admirable traits and annoying quirks. But Jax was right. He'd only known John as the quiet, loving father, a sliver of the whole of the man. "He is so proud of you, Jackson Scott."

"Was. Maybe," Jax said bitterly.

"Is. Definitely," Phoebe argued. "Trust me. If he's proud of you, then he loves me, and I'm not ready for any of that to be past tense."

Jax gave a tight nod and let out a breath. "Okay. Yeah. I get that."

"Good. Now, do me a favor. Go find Beckett and make sure he's not managing and orchestrating. Piss him off if you have to. But I want him to have a little room to feel tonight, okay?"

Jax gave her another hug. "It will give me great pleasure to piss him off."

They broke apart, and Phoebe took a step backwards.

"Mom, you gonna tell me why you have two forks in your pocket and a bottle of booze in your hand?"

Guilty, Phoebe chewed on her lip. "Because..."

"Because what?"

"Because I said so?"

"That didn't work when we were kids."

"I was kind of hoping you'd cut me a break and let it work just for tonight."

"What kind of cake did she bring?" Jax asked. Her youngest, with the barbed wit and mischievous nature, always managed to surprise her with his moments of quiet soulfulness. The longing in her son's eyes had nothing to do with cake and everything to do with the woman who'd made it.

"Pineapple upside down."

"Make sure she knows she's welcome here, okay?"

"I will," Phoebe promised, relieved.

He gave her a wink. "I'm gonna go spill something greasy on Beckett's shirt."

"Jax?"

He stopped, his hands shoved in his pockets, shoulders hunched. "Yeah, Mom?"

"I love you."

"Love you, too."

～

"WHERE'D you have to go for booze? Canada? I was getting ready to dig in with my hands," Joey griped. She was sitting on a hay bale, her long legs swinging in time to the Wild Nigels' thumping beat outside. The cake was uncovered and ready for consuming. Phoebe slid onto the bale on the other side of the cake plate and handed over a fork.

"I got waylaid by someone."

Joey's shoulders stiffened, and Phoebe guessed she knew who had done the waylaying.

Phoebe twisted open the bottle and took a deep drink. "Ah." She wiped her mouth with her sleeve still damp from tears—so many tears—and handed the bottle to Joey. Phoebe plunged her fork into the yellow spongey cake.

"If you ever get tired of school and horses, I'll set you up with a bakery," Phoebe said with her mouth full of sugary perfection.

"Mmm," Joey said, passing the bottle back and digging in. "Think I'll stick with horses. I'd hate dealing with customers," she shuddered.

"You know you're welcome out there. I don't want you to think that you can't grieve with us because of what happened between you and Jax."

Joey flinched at his name, and Phoebe, feeling like an asshole, took another drink.

"No," Joey said, shaking her head. "I don't want him or anybody to see me like... this."

"Like what?" Phoebe prodded gently.

Joey's eyes clouded. She bit her trembling lower lip. "He was a really good man," she said finally, choking the words out.

They weren't talking about Jax anymore.

"Oh, my sweet girl. John considered you family, and so do I," Phoebe said. She wanted to reach out to the girl to hug her until the hurt went away. But Joey shifted as if reading her intentions.

"I loved him. A lot," she said with a shuddering breath.

"We all love you, Joey. All of us. Don't feel like you need to go through this alone, please. That will make this worse for me, worse for all of us."

"I have something for you," Joey said, letting out a shuddering breath.

"Besides cake?" Phoebe teased.

Joey leaned to the side and pulled an envelope from her back pocket. "Here."

Phoebe caught her breath when she saw the handwriting on the back.

My Phoebe.

"Where did you get this?" Phoebe asked, her throat tight as she traced the letters of her name as written by her husband.

"Middle of the night last night. I knew you all were home, so I went in and sat with John for a while," Joey confessed.

Phoebe squeezed Joey's knee. "Thank you for that."

"He made me promise to give it to you after... after. You're not going to read it right now and go to pieces, are you?"

Phoebe stared at the envelope and then pressed it to her heart. "No, I think I'll wait a little while."

Joey nodded in relief. "He was a good man," she said again, making a neat row of fork holes in the cake.

"He made three other really good men, too," Phoebe said, reaching out and squeezing Joey's hand.

Joey snorted. "Well, two out of three ain't bad."

31

The wake was never going to end. It was already midnight, and someone had the brilliant idea to pull the hay wagon out to use as a makeshift stage. Neighbor after neighbor had taken the stage to share their favorite stories about John, and then the Wild Nigel's had launched back into their playlist. The food had been replenished by dozens and dozens of pizzas and subs from town. She didn't know how it was happening, but every time her glass was empty, someone filled it back up again.

There were eleven children sound asleep in her living room while their parents continued to "mourn" in spectacular Blue Moon fashion.

The entire municipality was just going to party itself to death, and at this point, Phoebe was okay with that. And just when she thought things couldn't get weirder, someone brought her a goat.

"This yours?"

Ellery, a sweetheart of a teenager who was going through an unfortunate goth phase, clomped over in her knee-high platform boots. The goat chewed at the party streamer someone had tied loosely around its neck.

Phoebe had no idea where the goat or the party streamer came from. She shook her head. "I've never seen that goat before in my life."

The goat bleated and dug at the ground with one dainty foot.

Ellery pressed her lips together, her black lipstick forming a dash on her pale face. "What should we do with her? I think it's a her. She has long lashes and little feet."

The goat's yellow eyes fixed on Jax as he wandered by, a slice of pizza in his hand. Before anyone could react, the goat snatched the pizza out of his grip, her ears and tail twitching as she devoured the pineapple and olive.

"What the—" Jax peered at the goat. "Did we get a goat?"

Phoebe shrugged. "I guess so. Ellery, can you put her in with Leopold at the front of the barn before she eats everyone else's pizza? He'll probably like the company."

"Sure!" Ellery clomped off with the goat in tow.

Only in Blue Moon would a goat crash a party, Phoebe thought.

The Wild Nigels ended their song to tremendous applause from the nowhere near sober audience.

Fran, the twenty-year-old band leader with a purple Mohawk that matched the flames on her wheelchair, leaned into her microphone. "This next one's before our time, but it's a little something we've been working on for John for his wedding anniversary. This one's for you, Phoebe." Fran pointed pistol fingers at Phoebe. "Guys, I'm gonna need your help with this one."

Phoebe's sons, all three of them, a little the worse for wear due to whatever alcohol had been flowing like Niagara Falls took the stage. Well, Carter staggered onto it. Beckett tripped over it, and Jax climbed him like a mountain goat before dragging his inebriated brother onto the stage.

Phoebe's shoulders shook with suppressed laughter. She pulled Mrs. Nordemann's cloak of mourning—a gift along with the woman's special tofu kale casserole—a little tighter around her shoulders. And as the first strains of "Do You Really Want to Hurt Me?" poured out, she hooted. A thousand memories of that first summer flooding through her.

It was a beginning in the end, and it was beautiful.

Her boys crowded around the microphone for the chorus, and Phoebe grinned up into the dark sky where the stars twinkled just as they always had and the navy blue of night clung like a soft blanket.

She brought her fingertips to her lips and blew a kiss heavenward.

32

Present Day

*L*ovingly, Phoebe tucked John's essay back into the envelope. She'd read John's goodbye at least a thousand times in the first year without him. And every year since then, she revisited it, remembering the unforgettable man.

She dabbed at her eyes with another tissue and gulped down some wine to ease the tightness in her throat. *It was amazing, the things the human heart could contain,* she mused. The joy, the grief, the peace, and the strife. The shelves above her were a testament to that. Loosely organized in chronological order, the mismatched frames and their images told the story of a life full of love and loss, joy, and the underlying satisfaction that carried through it all.

Her first wedding day picture, in a whitewashed wood frame, showed her standing hand in hand with John saying their vows against a backdrop of sunflowers that went on forever. There were baby pictures of the boys, kindergarten and Cub Scouts, prom and sports. John and the boys. The farm as it had been back on the day she'd arrived. There were her sons' weddings and the babies and not-so babies.

Her second wedding picture resided in a lovely filigree frame, one of her in Franklin's arms on the dance floor, laughing at something wonderful. Deliriously happy again. Wasn't it strange that she could remember both wedding days so perfectly in high-definition detail? She felt like the same person who stepped foot on this farm in 1985, yet so much had changed within and without.

Her sons had deemed Franklin a man among men—at least after their initial shock that Phoebe was indeed dating. Together, she and Franklin had taken their two families and joined them in ways that could never be undone.

Franklin supported and encouraged her to remember John, to keep him an integral part of their blended family. And she loved him all the more for it. He made her laugh every single day with his wicked sense of humor, and Phoebe knew John would approve of her choice. And through Franklin, Phoebe finally got the girls she'd wished for. Her step-daughters were smart, sweet, and strong, and she loved them as fiercely as she did her own sons.

It was a beautiful life so far, and she couldn't wait to see what was next.

Phoebe counted her lucky stars every damn day that she got to love the two best men in the world and raise three more. The tears were dry, and her smile wide. Somedays, the gratitude she felt for her life overwhelmed her.

Life was hard, but that's what made it so incredibly good. That's what made her appreciate every second that she had on this earth. Even on the darkest day, there was still beauty to see, still love to find. There was still a beginning to find in every end. She knew that now and hoped that her family knew it, too.

She heard the screen door swing open at the front of the house and a chorus of "Mom!"

Her boys, men now—husbands and fathers—trooped inside. All tall and dark. Beckett impeccably dressed as always, hair neatly trimmed. Carter, with his thick beard, and Jax, in rumpled flannel, leaned more toward casual.

But they were all handsome as sin and wore it with an easy confidence. They looked happy, healthy, relaxed. A farmer, a lawyer, and a screenwriter, all running a brewery named after their father.

We did good, John, Phoebe said silently, sending the message up to the heavens.

"Oh, great. She's drinking already," Jax joked.

"You try raising three boys in a barn and see if you don't start drinking," Phoebe reminded him.

"I'm dealing with an eighteen-year-old, a seven-year-old, and Joey," Jax said. "I may join you." He took her glass and gulped it down.

Phoebe laughed, her heart full and light. "That's why you're my favorite," she told him, patting his arm.

Carter leaned down and kissed her on the top of the head. "Happy Birthday, Mom."

"Thank you, sweetie. Ignore what I said to Jax. You're my favorite," she said in a stage whisper.

"Hollywood can't be the favorite," Beckett argued. "Neither can Wookiee face here. I'm the lowest maintenance son. That makes me the favorite by default."

Phoebe gave him a kiss on the cheek. "You're absolutely right, Beckett. You're my favorite. Although, you do know that you have a beard now, too, right?"

"Yeah, who's the Wookiee face now, Mr. Mayor?" Carter said, giving his brother a shove.

Beckett knocked into the glass bowl of fruit on the counter, arguing about how much better his beard was than Carter's.

"Oh, for Pete's sake," Phoebe cut in. "Take me to lunch before someone goes through the drywall."

THEY TOOK her to Villa Harvest where the hostess led them to a long table under a festive umbrella on the patio where it looked as though half the town was enjoying lunch.

"Happy Birthday, Phoebe," Mrs. Nordemann, still in her all black mourning gear eight years after the death of Mr. Nordemann, called out cheerily from her table with Bobby from Peace of Pizza. They raised their glasses to her, and Phoebe blew them a kiss.

The greetings were the same at every table. She knew every single person here. Blue Moon had always been that kind of place. The town had accepted her as one of their own and never let her down. Looking around the patio, she realized she was surrounded by people who loved her without biological requirement. They were men and women who cheered next to her at high school track meets, who held her hand and baked her horrible casseroles in the weeks after John passed, who danced at her wedding to Franklin.

People who knew the names of her grandchildren, business owners who had given her bookkeeping work when times were tight on the farm. An entire town of friends who had raised enough money to rescue her own parents—strangers to them—from crippling debt.

Hell, she was going to cry again.

"How did we rate such a big table?" Phoebe asked, taking a seat on the striped cushion.

"Pretty sure the owner has a thing for you, Mom," Beckett teased.

She picked up the menu on her plate. "Phoebe's Day Specials," she read.

"He definitely has a thing for you." Carter winked over his own menu.

Franklin appeared on the patio, and Phoebe enjoyed the stumble her heart took as it did every time she saw her husband. He wore a new Hawaiian shirt, this one white with red and pink hearts everywhere. He was a bear of a man in size but a teddy bear in character. There was nothing Franklin Merrill wouldn't do for her or for anyone for that matter. He loved fiercely and was a soft spot to land for anyone who needed one.

"For my favorite stepsons," Franklin said, whipping a basket of fresh bread sticks and steaming marinara from behind his back. Her sons pounced on it as if they hadn't eaten in weeks.

"And for my beautiful bride," Franklin professed. The lunch crowd "awh-ed" as he swept a massive bouquet from behind his back.

Phoebe's breath caught at the sight of them. At least a dozen sunflowers mixed in with wildflowers of every color.

"Oh, Franklin," she breathed. Her heart squeezed.

"I saw them in the window at Every Bloomin' Thing and thought they looked like you—beautiful and just a little wild."

"Oh," she said again, sniffling. *Sunflowers, of course.*

"If Mom starts crying or you two start making out, I'm out of here," Jax threatened.

"Before cannoli?" Franklin grinned.

"Of course, not! After cannoli. I'm not an idiot."

"Yes, you are," Carter and Beckett chimed in.

Jax kicked both his brothers under the table. But Phoebe was too happy, her heart too full, to yell at them.

"Are you joining us for lunch?" she asked her husband hopefully.

"I think my boss will allow me to take my lunch break," Franklin winked. "In fact, I think we're all joining you."

He whistled through his fingers, and everyone on the patio rose from their seats.

The table that had been hidden behind a palm dropped their menus and Phoebe clapped her hands over her mouth. Michael, Hazel, and Donovan Cardona grinned at her.

And as an off-key rendition of "Happy Birthday" began, the Pierce girls appeared at the patio gate. Joey and Summer, each holding three bottles of champagne worked their way toward her. They were followed by Gia, Emma, and Eva— reliving their restaurant days working for their father— carrying trays of delicate stemware.

Elvira, her dearest friend in the world, was last in the procession carrying a cake that had entirely too many candles on it.

Franklin kissed Phoebe's knuckles as the song reached its blaring crescendo.

She stood and looked around the patio crowded with her wonderful family and friends. Anthony Berkowicz, son of Rainbow and Gordon and the lone employee of *The Monthly Moon,* jumped out from behind a palm and blinded her with the flash from his camera. Joey shoved him back behind the plant. Nikolai, her other handsome step-son-in-law, stepped forward with his professional camera and grinned at her before capturing the moment.

"I don't know how to thank each and every one of you for the role you've played in making my life so wonderful. I don't know if I ever can. But I do know this, I'm grateful for you all every single day. You're more than friends and neighbors. You're family, and I'm so lucky to have you. And now I'm going to sit back down before I start blubbering."

There was laughter and applause and a few tears from the crowd, her family.

As the cake was cut, the bubbly popped and poured, Franklin cupped her face in his big hands. "Happy birthday, my lovely wife."

He kissed her lightly, sweetly, and even then, her heart sang with the joy of a woman who was truly, deeply loved.

AUTHOR'S NOTE TO THE READER

Dear Reader,

This was a book I had no intention of writing. A couple of readers came up with the idea, and I couldn't figure out how to write John and Phoebe's love story without dimming Phoebe's marriage with adorable, sweet, Hawaiian shirt aficionado Franklin. And then I realized it happens in real life all the time.

The human heart doesn't contain a finite amount of love that can only be doled out sparingly. It's made to love big and hard and wild all the years of your life, and those kooky Blue Mooners really get that.

Writing this story that I hadn't intended on writing was such an amazing journey because I got to see how many links existed running back and forth between the generations. Phoebe showing up on the farm ready to work and write was the same a generation later for Summer and Carter. John's reluctance to do the "wrong" thing is ingrained in Beckett, and Jax and the way he expresses himself is just like his father.

The Blue Moon books are about family. They're also about

hot, steamy, hilarious romance, but they're mainly about family.

If you'd like more behind-the-scenes gibberish from me or want to stay up-to-date with what I'm cooking or drinking or you have a great book idea you'd like to feed me, visit me on Facebook, Instagram or sign up for my awesome newsletter.

Thanks again for reading, and I hope you'll check out the rest of my books.

Xoxo,
  Lucy

Made in the USA
Middletown, DE
16 March 2024

51586334R00156